A Pitif

When Christine has her baby, she seems to have left the rest of the world behind. Is anyone on her side? Not the baby's father – she hates him anyway. Not her father. All he cares about is what the neighbours think. She knows her mum is trying but it's so difficult for her. When her parents come to collect her, nobody talks all the way home. How can she go back to living there like a child? And how can she face life alone with the new baby?

Christine's story is one of five hard-hitting stories about young people in Britain today.

JAN NEEDLE

A Pitiful Place

A Magnet Book

First published 1984 by André Deutsch Ltd
This Magnet edition published 1985
by Methuen Children's Books Ltd
11 New Fetter Lane, London EC4P 4EE
Copyright © 1984 Jan Needle
Printed in Great Britain by
Richard Clay (The Chaucer Press) Ltd,
Bungay, Suffolk

ISBN 0 416 50400 0

For Jane and Nick

Contents

Given to Tears 9

A Letter From Wally 63

No Lady, Godiva 76

The Ghost of Mrs Hitler 94

A Pitiful Place to Die 110

Given To Tears

ONE

CHRISTINE SPALDING was still at school when she got pregnant, but by the time she had the baby she was finished. In fact, she was in hospital giving birth when her classmates were having a good time on their last day at St Edward's comp. They got little presents from each other, and the teachers who liked them, and Christine got a baby. Sharon. Seven pounds three ounces, lots of black hair and a screwed-up little red face. Most of her friends weren't all that chuffed to be leaving school and facing up to the harsh realities of life outside, but Christine was overjoyed. She had Sharon.

It was her happiness, her total lack of apparent worry about the future, that started all the trouble again, peculiarly. Because it seemed to make her father mad, to reopen all the old wounds she thought had healed. From the very moment he saw the little baby, and Christine's joyful face shining over it in the hospital, something seemed to go wrong. It was resentment, he was angry that she should be so glad, and instead of being happy himself at the birth of his granddaughter, she could see that her father was embittered. He held himself in check, in the hospital, he made the usual noises of delight, but it was a struggle. Christine looked at her mum, frightened, and her mum smiled a tight, anxious smile. She could feel it too. They both tried to play it very cool.

When Christine had admitted she was pregnant, there'd

been awful scenes. She couldn't remember them in detail, probably because she did not want to, but for weeks on end her life had been disastrous. Her father was a respectable man, as he told her until she was nauseous, and the discovery that his daughter, his little girl, his pride and joy, was a slut, a tart, a whore . . . oh, the scenes were terrible. Her mother, inevitably Chris supposed, had stood by her from the first, and fought her father (sometimes physically, to Christine's undying horror) all along the line. And it had been a traditional one, that line. She was to be thrown out ('Over my dead body' – Mum). To have an abortion (over Christine's ditto). To have the little bastard adopted – anything, in fact, to ease Dad's shame. He was a respectable man, a buyer, who had once almost stood for the council. What would the neighbours say?

It was the neighbours, in fact, who had caused some of the worst of the nastiness. For Christine, they were the supreme irrelevance, and the supreme insult. Her father, it appeared, was prepared to sacrifice fifteen years of love, of trust, of comradeship, for fear of what the neighbours would say! Any feelings of shame that she may have secretly had (*did*, naturally) were turned to fury and rebellion by this apparent monstrosity. Sod the neighbours, she screamed one night. Bugger the neighbours. *Balls* to the neighbours. Her father had hit her, her mother had hit her father, the place had been turned into a screaming shambles. And the neighbours, no doubt, had listened at the walls, in amazement and satisfaction, or both. Who knew?

A pre-emptive strike by her mother cut the neighbours-problem down to size. The ruling from Dad was bound to be – soon – that the neighbours must never know. So she told them, the day after the row. In private, up and down the terraced street, the news must have been chewed over with gusto, but in public, the neighbours behaved politely, pretending indifference, or offering, mildly, sympathy and understanding. For her father, the problem was diminished, but for Christine, although she could not precisely say why, it got worse. She never forgave the neighbours for their hypocrisy. She hated them for being sympathetic – as if she needed sympathy! – and she was convinced that they thought she was a slag. Their friendly, understanding, smiles made her feel, for the first time, that she ought to be ashamed. She could hardly bear to be polite to them.

With the pressure of respectability off his shoulders, though – she had to admit – Dad got better. He still didn't like it, and he used to make infuriating remarks about what a blessing it was that none of the grandparents were still alive to see it, and so on. But over the months that followed her terrified announcement of the impending happy event, he calmed down, and got back to normal, and tried to repair some of the damage he had done. By the time Christine went into the Royal to have the child he was – on the surface – quite happy about it. When she saw how he'd responded to the actual birth, Christine had a muscular spasm in her stomach. She was sick with fright. Please God don't let it all start up again.

She did not see him for two days after that, but it became immediately clear, on the drive home, that her father was having a losing battle with his resentment, or rekindled anger, or whatever exactly it was. She sat in the back, cuddling Sharon, and her mother sat in the front with Dad. Christine kept her head down, she hardly spoke, but the atmosphere was dreadful. There was something in the way he held his neck; it was tense, at a slightly odd angle. Once she caught a sight of his face in the driving mirror, and it was strained, with a brooding tightness around the eyes.

They got home without incident, however, and turned into the road. Then it was Christine's turn to feel tension. The rows of familiar brick houses looked different, unfriendly. Every window, in her imagination if not in fact, hid a peering, secret, face. Every curtain twitched. She realised, with a shock, that she was squeezing Sharon to her chest, much too hard. Her arms ached as she consciously eased the pressure.

It came to a head when they got out of the car to go into the house. Christine, the new mum, was getting onto the pavement awkwardly, too many arms and legs to get through the narrow gap. Mum was holding a bundle of blankets, trying to help and getting in the way. Dad had walked up the short path to the front door and was putting his key in the lock, looking furtive. Next door's front door opened and Mrs Leggatt came out. She had a smile on her face that looked as false as hell, and she had a jolly ring to her voice that was ten times falser.

'Oh hello,' she said. 'I just popped out to welcome you back, Christine. I just popped out to look at baby.'

Chris was standing in the gateway, hot and bothered. She'd banged Sharon's forehead against the door-pillar getting out and made a mark. Her father's face, behind Mrs Leggatt who was walking down to meet her, was a picture of resentment and dislike. Something in Christine gave up.

'Oh piss off, Mrs Leggatt,' she said. 'Why don't you leave me alone.'

Mrs Leggatt stopped. Her face fell. She went bright red.

'Christine!' roared her father.

He stood still for a second, then took two or three staggering, stiff-legged steps towards her. Christine stepped backwards and knocked into her mother, who was close behind. Her mother dropped the baby blankets and Christine almost fell. As her father lifted his hand to smack her face, his eyes wide with anger, she lifted up the baby as protection. Mrs Leggatt shrieked.

The blow never landed. Christine jumped to one side and scuttled past her dad through the front door. Her mother pushed him furiously, violently, and he turned and followed Christine. Her mother bent to pick up the blankets, then glanced fearfully at the door and hurried after them. The door slammed and Mrs Leggatt was alone. She looked at the curtains in the terrace opposite. She looked at the pile of blankets on the path. She looked at the car door, hanging open across the pavement. She smiled weakly and went indoors.

It was a bad row, the worst for many months, and in its aftermath Sally Gerrold turned up. Christine's mother opened the door to her, and averted her puffy, tear-streaked face. She did not say hello, just nodded to the stairs, and Sally understood. The house was quiet, and she did not ask where Mr Spalding was. She left her briefcase in the hall and climbed to Christine's bedroom.

Sally Gerrold was a social worker, who had come, so to speak, with the baby. Because Christine was still at school, and not sixteen, when she had got pregnant, the people at the ante-natal clinic had 'referred' her. Sally Gerrold had turned up, luckily, only about three months ago, after most of the family friction had died down. It had been made clear that the baby was going to be born, and was going to be kept, and there were no decisions to be made. She'd interviewed them all a couple of times, made notes, and rung occasionally to see if there were any problems. There were not.

Not until now. Sally Gerrold knocked quietly, then entered Christine's bedroom. It was dark, with the curtains drawn, and the only noise in it was sniffing. Christine was lying on the bed, with her head under the pillow. She had always cried like that, ever since she'd been a little girl. She wriggled when the door opened, tried to bury herself in the mattress, but she did not speak.

'Hello,' said Sally Gerrold. 'It's me, Sally. Shall I open the curtains?'

Christine did not reply, so Sally walked carefully across the room and drew the curtains back. As the light streamed in there was a movement from the other side of Christine's bed. There was a cot there, with Sharon in it, and Sharon stirred. But she did not wake. She had been as good as gold, in fact, throughout. She had slept through everything. She had missed her first full family quarrel.

It was some time before Chris would come out from beneath the pillow, and it was longer before she had completely stopped sniffling and crying. She sat awkwardly on her own bed, in her own house, being talked to by a stranger. It seemed wrong.

It also seemed wrong, though – much more wrong – that things had turned out this way. It was her homecoming, her big day, and Dad had spoiled it all. The bedroom had been done up, she and Mum had had hours of fun organising the cot, and the nappies, and the changing-mat and everything, and then all this. As she thought about it her misery and resentment overflowed and she started to talk, to tell Sally just what a bastard he had been, how he'd always hated her, ever since she'd confessed, and how it was finally coming out, his true, his lousy rotten colours. She went on and on.

Sally Gerrold sat and listened, hardly making a sound. Every now and then she made a noise like 'mm', and occasionally she clicked her tongue in sympathy. After quite a long time she took out a Kleenex and dabbed her client's face, then a little later she put her arm around her. Christine rested her head, briefly, on Sally Gerrold's shoulder, and noted the smell of new wool and a perfume that was so elusive that it must be quite expensive, way above her class. She was very comforted. She went to the bathroom and had a pee and washed her face and returned. Sally Gerrold was looking down at Sharon, who still slept peacefully.

14

'She's a lovely little girl,' she said. 'What are you calling her?'

Christine smiled shyly.

'Sharon,' she said. 'I thought I told you, last time. I've always wanted to have a little girl called Sharon. It's a lovely name.'

'Ah,' said Sally. 'I thought you may have changed your mind. Now let's sit down again, Chris, and talk this over, this thing about your dad. I don't want to get you het up again, but you've got to see his side, you know. You've got to live together, after all. Come and sit back down.'

Christine felt resentment at her father's name, but it did not last. She sat down in a chair and Sally sat opposite. That in itself made Chris feel good, and mature, and grown-up – to have a chair to offer to a friend. It made her feel like a proper woman, like a mother. With no rotten *father*, she thought rather smugly, to come and put a spanner in the works! She'd have to get a kettle up here, she thought, an electric one and some cups, so that she could make them coffee, people who came visiting. Perhaps Dad would pay to have a tap laid on, a little basin in the corner.

You couldn't feel resentment very long, with Sally Gerrold, Christine quickly realised. After the hysteria and the nastiness, she was calm, and sensible, and nice. She understood Christine's side, Christine couldn't deny it. But she also knew what made her father tick, apparently. She explained that his new anger, the smouldering anger that kept bursting through, was completely natural, predictable. That was why, she said, she had chosen this day, the day of Christine's return from hospital, to visit. She'd thought there might have been a row.

'But it's not *fair*,' said Christine. 'I was looking forward to it. I was bringing little Sharon back to her *home*. And he went on like that.'

'Yes,' said Sally. 'But that's probably it, you see. You

15

were bringing the baby back here as if you owned the place. You probably seemed to him to think so, anyway. He'd got used to the idea of you being pregnant, and that was bad enough for him, then there's the baby there, in your arms, as large as life, and you're *still* not the slightest bit repentant. He probably felt ashamed, Christine. He probably felt sick with worry about what the neighbours would think. And you – no doubt – just sat there grinning. Like a cat with two tails.'

Christine had flushed at the part about the neighbours, so Sally, guessing she'd scored a hit, waited for her to confess. When Chris told her what she'd said to Mrs Leggatt, she nodded, earnestly.

'It is a little bit selfish of you, Chris,' she said. 'I don't want to criticise, but you have been a weeny bit insensitive, you know. Your father's probably been living under quite a lot of strain over all this business.'

After they'd talked for a while longer, Sally said they had to patch it up. Christine argued, but it was no good. Sally told her to smarten up, while she – Sally – went to talk downstairs. It was half an hour before she called Christine down, and the three of them, mother, father and daughter, faced each other in the living room. Mum looked better – not good but better – and Dad looked at the floor. Christine, at Sally's instigation, apologised, and Mum started to cry once more. Mr Spalding, awkwardly, put his arm around his wife, and Christine promptly burst into tears. Sally Gerrold waited for a minute or two to let the emotional flow get well under way, then she quietly left. The reconciliation, it was clear, was a success.

Christine, later, lay on her bed and experienced a mixture of relief and fear. She had fed and changed Sharon, who had gone to sleep again, and she could hear the comforting sound of the television down below. The reconciliation had been an emotional success, certainly, they had kissed and

16

made it up. But she still feared, somehow, that it might turn out to be a false dawn. She sighed and yawned. She was exhausted.

Christine listened, with love, to her daughter's quiet, rapid breathing. Thank God for her, at any rate. She'd slept through everything.

She was going to be good, thought Christine sleepily. As good as she was beautiful. Thank God for that. She slept.

It was a false dawn, in more than one way, although that did not become apparent for some time. Sharon slept all that night, and for several nights to come, with only brief interludes when she demanded to be fed, or changed. Some of the scare stories Christine had heard, from other mothers and her aunties, receded to the background of her mind, and she grew strong and healthy through contentment and unbroken nights. Her love for her baby, which had felt incredibly huge when she was born, to her amazement grew: which hardly seemed possible but was true. Her father, also, throve on the unbroken nights, aided perhaps by the fact that Mrs Leggatt accepted Chris's apology without reserve, gave her some lovely baby clothes and a box of chocolates two days later, and made it perfectly plain that neither she nor any of the other neighbours had anything but goodwill towards the unmarried mother and the little girl. The next time Sally Gerrold called, she was very pleased.

For a while, quite a long while, there was peace. Christine fairly quickly developed a routine, and the fact that her life was completely absorbed in the needs of a small, helpless thing did not bother her – she revelled in it. She fed and changed the baby, cuddled it and bathed it. She spent its waking hours making silly goo-goo noises at its face, she put her finger out for hour after hour to be gripped or waved at.

17

The only time there was any friction in the house – and it did not happen often – was when her mother wanted (and Christine wanted it as well) to 'look after' the baby, do the nappy-washing, that sort of thing. Mr Spalding was dead against it, and he dug his heels in. It was their grand-daughter, yes. But it was Christine's baby, and she must care for it: in every way. It wasn't fair on Mum ('I don't mind, Ted. I *want* to!') and he wasn't having it. Neither Christine nor her mother quite understood why he was so deter-mined, but they did not try to fight it hard. He was a stubborn old devil, they agreed. But it didn't matter, much.

Sally visited once a week, and Christine began to look upon her almost as a friend, not as a social worker merely. Strangely, this feeling was increased, not diminished, by a sort of row they had.

It happened, completely unexpectedly, at the end of a routine visit. Admittedly, Christine had been feeling edgy when Sally had arrived, because of a little run-in she'd had with her dad over the radio. She got lonely for grown-up company occasionally, when she was in her room with Sharon all the time, and another one of Dad's 'things' was that she must not use the whole of the house the whole of the time. It was like her mum not helping with the baby, he insisted: they were a family, but Christine and Sharon were a family as well. He and Mum were grandparents, and they had their own life to live, and they needed to be separate from time to time. It sounded quite sensible at first, until she started to get lonely, then Christine began to brood on how her life had changed. Only a few months ago, less than a year for God's sake, the 'family' had been her and her mum and dad. Now he was saying they had to be apart. It wasn't logical – she thought – nor was it fair. How could he and Mum be 'grandparents' now, and separate, when just a little time ago they'd been her mum and dad? So in her room,

18

sometimes, she played Radio One or the local pop station a sight too loud, on purpose (to be noticed, and to drive the blues away) and the night before, her dad had moaned because he wanted to watch the telly and said he couldn't hear the voices.

The spat with Sally had nothing to do with this whatever, but was part of her sense of isolation. Christine felt low, and just a teeny bit lost, and she felt ugly and horrible at the same time. She'd gone spotty, on and off, since Sharon had been born, and constipated, and her hair was still dull and lifeless, just like in the ads. Sally, as usual, was well turned out and cool, and wearing clothes that were smart, and subtle, and expensive. She wasn't exactly good-looking, or attractive, but she looked smooth and self-contained, and she made Chris feel lumpy, and lower class, and vulgar. Awkward was the word. She made Chris look awkward.

Christine had told Sally about the radio business, and Sally, as usual, had been all sweet reason. It irritated Chris a lot, sometimes, the way she saw both sides of everything. She suggested that Chris was being a shade unfair, and how would she like it if her father played the television so loudly that she could not hear her music? Chris responded grumpily: 'But TV's so *boring*, Sally. They just go on and on at the same thing all the time. You've got to have one foot in the grave to watch TV, it's all the bloody same.'

Sally put down her coffee cup and smiled. The smile struck Christine, all at once, as dead superior, and patronising.

'Well I must admit,' she said, 'that Radio One strikes me as ten times worse than television. If we're going to talk about being boring, pop music takes the biscuit for my money.' She gestured towards Sharon, who was lying in her cot staring at a line of rattling beads on an elastic string. 'Think of the baby, Christine. I hope you're planning something better for her than a diet of non-stop drivel.'

19

Christine began to see red. She could not help herself. Her voice went up a notch.

'I'll be the judge of that, thanks very much,' she said. '*I* happen to think that music's good for . . . And I happen to think that telly . . .' She stopped, feeling trapped and lumpy, and stupid. 'And anyway,' she blurted out. 'Why don't you ever call my baby by her proper name? You've never called her Sharon once, not ever. Why?'

Whether it was coincidence, or if she'd been shouting or whatever, the door opened then and her mum came in. Sally was talking, still with total reasonableness, although her smile had become a trifle fixed.

'Oh, you've noticed, have you?' she was saying. She tried a little chuckle. 'Well, you're very quick, Christine, I must say. To be honest, it's *not* my favourite name. I've always thought it was . . . sort of . . .'

'Cow! You cow!' shouted Christine. In front of her mother's horrified eyes she burst into tears. She sprang to her feet and dashed out of the room. Sally and Mrs Spalding were left looking at each other. For a moment the only noise was the rattling of the baby's beads. Then Sally Gerrold laughed.

'Poor Chris,' she said. 'She's very tense. I hope she doesn't walk out on the baby often.'

'No,' said Mrs Spalding. 'Of course she doesn't, love. I don't know what's got into her.'

Downstairs, they heard the front door slam.

'Oh,' said Sally Gerrold. 'She's gone out.'

Mrs Spalding walked to the window and glanced through.

'She'll be back,' she said. 'She's only a kid. I expect it all gets on top of her sometimes.' She looked at Sally's face, rather embarrassed. 'That what you said just now, love,' she said, tentatively. 'About little Sharon's name. You didn't . . . I mean . . . Did you mean it, like?'

20

Sally smoothed down her skirt as she stood up to go. She seemed to be choosing what to say.

'No, of course not,' she said brightly. 'It's just a habit of mine, not using children's names. I see so many of them, you see, in my job. No, Sharon's . . . it's very nice.'

That night Christine's Mum was extra pleasant to her daughter, but it got her nowhere. Chris was petulant, and childish, and resentful. And terrified about her row with the social worker. She shut herself in her room early, and played the radio defiantly loud for half an hour or so until she got ashamed, then went to bed to cry herself to sleep. But little Sharon had other ideas. She decided to cry as well, and she kept it up all night – loud, insistent, piercing. That, strangely, was really the end of the false dawn, because from then on she became a night-disaster. Instead of long, unbroken hours of sleep, Christine frequently got long, unbroken hours of wakefulness. She got paler, and tireder, and less resilient. But she coped. She squared her shoulders, and gritted her teeth, and got down to it. The joys of motherhood.

Sally was great about the row, and from then on Christine's sense of a real friendship developing between them got stronger and stronger. The very next time she visited, Sally told her she recognised how difficult certain things must be for her, and not to worry if she ever blew her top. She must feel very isolated, she said, and asked her if she ever saw her old friends, or missed them. Christine said she hardly ever did, and when she met a girl-friend from her schooldays in the street it could be quite embarrassing. She did not know why, but her friends got giggly, and silly, when they saw her with a baby, and after cuddling Sharon for a while would sort of slink off to a coffee place, looking dead relieved. They all struck Chris as being incredibly young now, as well, and obsessed with fashion and boys. Christine, who at school had been a pretty wild dresser, had settled down to jeans and tops and practically nothing else. They were useful with the baby, because you could have plenty of them and they were easy to change when you got mucked or sicked on.

It wasn't the whole story, of course, and as the weeks went by, Christine got to be more honest. She did get lonely, very very lonely, and she had begun to miss some of her mates, and the good times, and the discos and the skating, and the parties. Not the boys, though, she'd pulled a shutter down on boys. She did not tell Sally Gerrold the full extent of that, because it worried her just how deep it went. She didn't want to know them any more, she was terrified of them. It was the times she missed, she said, and her girl-friends. For male company, Simon Le Bon, who lived up on her wall and was delicious, was more than enough. He was good-looking, and remote, and safe. He was made of coloured paper.

She started telling Sally all her secret thoughts out of a mixture of new trust – and resentment. Her parents occasionally got quite close to gloating, without meaning to, over the distance that had come between her and her former friends. It suited them down to the ground, inevitably – because it was her friends, in their eyes, who had got her into the mess that they had got her out of. Perhaps, she thought, it was the reason her father wouldn't let her mum help with the baby – because it kept Chris tied up constantly. Christine knew that circumstances were turning her into a woman, and she still longed, from time to time, to be a girl. But Sally was her friend. She could be told.

When she had got into the habit of talking about private things, Christine held very little back. She started telling of her loneliness, and she ended up by spilling out the story of her life. Sally Gerrold was a good listener – an expert listener – and Christine, because of her isolation, had got very self-absorbed. In many ways, on many areas, she was far too frank, although she never knew it. Occasionally, through her self-obsession, she noticed signs of . . . what? Not disapproval, exactly, Sally would never disapprove; but she asked probing questions, then sat back and listened to the answers, silently, with an earnest concentration that was almost unnatural. About sex, for instance. Did Christine have a lot of boys? Did she know who Sharon's father was? Did she love him? Would she have married him if he'd asked?

Christine tried to answer truthfully, but what came out was not entirely true. She got excited, high, during some of the sessions, and panicky at the same time. She said she enjoyed making love, and she'd done it lots of times, with several different boys, like all her girl-friends had. Of course she knew who Sharon's father was, though, and no, she wouldn't dream of marrying him. His name was Graham, and he was seventeen and he had big feet and he was stupid, just a one-night stand. All of this came tumbling out, and Christine thought, maybe, it was the truth. The trouble was, the more she talked about these things, and thought about them, and romanced in her mind, the less she could remember exactly what was true and what was wishful thinking. In fact, late one night after a session with Sally, she could only remember having done it with one boy once, and Graham, her boyfriend, the love of her young life, about fifteen times. She didn't think any of the other girls in her class had done it at all, whatever some of them said, and she hadn't enjoyed it even a little bit, not even before she'd thought she might be pregnant. She also admitted to herself that if Graham had asked her she'd have married him like a shot, when she'd been old enough. But far from asking her he'd said he wasn't the father, it could be any one of a dozen boys, and that she was well known as the fifth-form bike, Spalding the Slag. It was certainly true now, though, at least

23

and absolutely, that she wouldn't marry him! She'd like to see him rot in hell.

Although she didn't think that Sally would disapprove of anything, there were areas where she half-sensed she might be shocking her, where she might be on dicey ground. Christine, young and naive as she was, did not associate sex with girls like Sally Gerrold, it never occurred to her that she might do it, even, might be good at it, be experienced. She was too well turned out, too quiet and respectable. So from time to time she found herself giving sort of sex lessons, to the social worker, then catching something in her face that stopped her in her tracks. One time was when Sally had questioned her about doing it with so many boys. 'Oh it's all right,' Christine had replied. 'It doesn't matter who you do it with, and how much you do it. Just as long as you don't catch none of them diseases.' She had suddenly felt a fool, and shut her mouth.

One thing Sally was very pleased about, and very obviously, was Christine deciding not to marry just because she was pregnant. That was absolutely essential, she said, and very wise. But when Chris said her mum and dad had thought so too, Sally appeared put out. She questioned Christine closely about this, and raised her eyebrows. Chris was perturbed. Why should Sally be surprised, for God's sake? Her mum and dad wanted the best for her, despite Dad's worries over the neighbours and that. The one thing they had *never* suggested was that she should try to marry some spotty jerk who'd turned out to be a lying little shit on top of everything. She wondered, with a sudden chill, just what Sally thought of her parents – and, perhaps, of her. It was not a comfortable thought.

Perhaps Sally picked up the chill, for she changed the subject to marriage in general. Here, Chris was on much firmer ground. She rattled on quite happily about her plans and hopes for the future. Now she'd got her silly accident, her mess, out of the way, she was going to hang on until the right boy came along, however long it took. She even had a picture of him in her mind, and he was tall, and thin, and ever so romantic. They'd settle down in a lovely little cottage by the sea, or in the country, or maybe they'd go abroad, to Australia, or America, say, to a land of opportunity. Sally asked her if she didn't fancy picking up her education later on, or getting a good job, but Christine was scornful. She had one child already, she said, and it was lovely, and she wanted lots and lots and lots more. Anyway, a woman's place was at home, to make it nice for a man, and to make a lovely, peaceful place for the children to grow up in, loved and cared for. Didn't Sally think so?

Sally laughed. No, she said, she did not. She was twenty three, and she'd never felt the urge to get married, although her boyfriend wanted to. (Her boyfriend! That shook Chris.) She was just as happy living with him on and off, (that shook her even more!) and she had absolutely no intention of ever having kids.

'I'm a career woman,' she said. 'I'm not intending to waste the best years of my life looking after some man and a gaggle of demanding little brats, however loveable they might be. Thank God for contraception, I say. Which reminds me, Chris. We ought to talk seriously about that soon. Just in case you ever get your interest back. In boys.'

Christine's face was burning. She was scandalised. She wasn't going back on boys, she gabbled. Next time would be the last, the real thing, wedding bells. And she would *not*, *never* use a contraceptive with the boy she loved.

They smoothed it over, and Sally even apologised for upsetting her, which Christine, naturally, denied. Over a cup of coffee, with Christine calmed and soothed by making up a feed for Sharon, Sally Gerrold explained that she saw things differently, perhaps – perhaps because she was older. She said that women, in her view, had a duty to take themselves more seriously than they once would have done, and that they should not let themselves be used – or abused – body or mind; that even marriage should be looked at dispassionately, because men had a tendency to think it was designed solely for their benefit. Christine listened calmly enough, holding the bottle to her baby's mouth, but she did not take much in. She had a hollow sensation still, a sensation that she and her new-found friend were a million miles apart.

When Sally got up to go, she stood in front of Christine, a smile on her face.

'Look, Christine,' she said. 'I'm sorry, I scare you sometimes, don't I? You think I'm making judgements. Well I'm not. I know we're from different backgrounds, I know you think differently from me about some things, but I promise you –'

Sharon, lying across Christine's lap wearing only a woolly vest and a pair of socks, let fly a great quantity of urine.

'Shit!' cried Christine. 'The little bitch has pissed me jeans!'

Sally's smile grew tight.

'You know,' she said. 'I'm not so sure you ought to use language like that in front of the baby, Christine. And don't call females bitches, dear. It's so . . .'

Christine held Sharon to her with one hand and pressed the other – with the bottle in it – to her forehead.

'Oh piss off, Sal,' she said, despairingly. 'Please piss off and leave me on my own. *Please*. Go away.'

Sally Gerrold went. She was biting her lip.

Christine waited for the next visit in a state approaching terror. There had been, she was certain, a real understanding growing up between them, a real friendship. And she needed it, oh God she needed it. But incidents like this unnerved her terribly. They made her realise that she and

26

Sally lived in different worlds, for a start-off, that on some things they spoke a different language. She went hot and cold when she thought about the sex thing, for instance. She had talked to Sally like a Dutch uncle, she'd given her *advice*! And Sally had a boyfriend, and she lived with him, and used contraceptives. How could she have been so daft? How could she have been so *raw*? She'd made herself look a fool. She must make herself look a fool every time she opened her mouth, practically. Sally Gerrold must think she was an ignorant working class cow, and a smartarse to boot. She must despise her.

Her nervousness when Sally finally arrived, was so transparent that the ice had melted in thirty seconds flat. Sally, who had come in looking rather grim, took one look at her face and burst out laughing.

'Oh Chris!' she said. 'You look appalling! You look so miserable! I'm not going to eat you, love, honestly I'm not!'

Christine sat down, heavily.

'Crikey, Sal,' she said. 'I've been so terrified. I wanted to ring up and apologise, honest. I was so *rude*. You must think I'm such a *berk*. I'm so, so sorry.'

Sally sat on the side of her chair and put an arm around her shoulder.

'It's the strain, that's all,' she said. 'I understand it, Christine, that's my job. Don't let it worry you, dear. Just be natural with me, always. If you can't cope, I want to know, that's what I'm here for. I'd much rather you don't put on an act, I want to see you as you really are.'

'I can cope most of the time,' said Christine. 'But you know how it is. It gets on top of me. I sometimes think I'm going crazy, cooped up all the time like this. And then upsetting you like that. My only . . .'

She stopped. Sally Gerrold waited, looked at her bowed head.

'Your only friend, were you going to say?' she asked. 'Don't be afraid to tell the truth, Chris. I hope you do see me as a friend. It's important for the good of everyone, you know.'

'Well I do,' said Christine. She glanced up quickly, at Sally's face, then down. 'You are my friend, Sally. My only friend. I've been dead miserable, honest. I thought I'd put you off.'

Sally patted her on the shoulder, then got up.

'I'll put the kettle on,' she said. 'We'll have a cup of coffee, shall we?'

She had not said that she was Christine's friend, and Christine noticed it. She would have liked, desperately, to ask. If it was true. If they *were* friends or if she was, somehow, just a client. It was an awful thought, that made her want to pant, that maybe for Sally it was just a job routine, a professional thing, a professional friendship.

But Sally's smile, as she handed her her coffee, was warm enough, and open enough, and surely genuine. Christine did not dare to ask.

With the crisis over, Christine's life settled rapidly back into its old routine. Sally visited once a week, but not always on the same day or at the same time, which Mr Spalding said cynically was so that Chris could be caught out if she didn't keep her room clean or the baby well looked after. Christine flared up at this, and accused her father of being a nasty-minded sod, and not caring for her half as much as Sally did in any case. The row could have got quite unpleasant, but her mother got back from the shops and sorted them both out with a flea in their ears.

But the spat with Dad was symptomatic. More and more frequently they were snapping at each other, over the silliest things, and there was a lot of tension in the air. Dad started complaining about the noise the baby made, especially at

28

night, and about the nappies and the baby clothes that were always cluttering up the place in festoons. Sharon had nappy rash quite badly at this time, and Christine let her crawl or lie about without a nappy on, which led to accidents. Her mother and Chris rubbished any complaints that Mr Spalding had, and told him bluntly that he could moan about messes when he started clearing up himself – which he would never do. But it didn't help the general atmosphere.

One of the main causes was Christine's state of mind. Her loneliness, and her desire for something to happen in her life, had got steadily worse, to the point where she had tentatively – and rather foolishly, looking back on it – suggested to Sally that they go to a concert together. She knew that Sally's taste in music was not her own – however straight she pitched it for effect – so she pretended she liked a bit of classical and asked if Sally knew of any good orchestras that would be on one night. Sally had thrown her not by turning her down on musical grounds, but by disapproving of the thought of her leaving Sharon for an evening.

'But it's not even with a baby-sitter!' Christine, amazed, had said. 'I'll get me mum and dad to do it. Dad won't mind, for once.'

But Sally had said, quite calmly, that it wasn't the same, was it? And Chris – almost in despair – had almost blurted out: 'Well I've got to get away from the little cow sometimes, haven't I?' Almost, but not quite. You didn't call females cows or bitches, she remembered. She was learning. But no babysitting? That, she could not comprehend.

The radio row had rumbled on and off, and her mother had pleaded with her, to keep the peace, to watch telly with them in the evenings when Sharon was asleep. She did, night after night, but with a strong and growing sense of frustration. For one thing, her mother and her father argued over what they ought to watch, which was boring and depressing in itself, and for another, whatever they finally hit on was rubbish, to her mind. She just could not believe how dull most television was, how ridiculous were the panel games, how predictable the soap operas, how boring the musical shows. Even the adverts, which most people reckoned were the best bits, palled after you'd seen them three or four times . . . then you had to endure them a thousand times more.

It all blew up one evening when her father was watching some documentary on a new miracle drug. He couldn't have been that interested, because he got up halfway through and went out to the kitchen, where Mum was making a pot of tea and some snacks. After he'd been gone a few minutes, Christine idly switched over to a different channel to see if there was anything more lively. Almost as if he'd been waiting for it to happen, Dad came back from the kitchen.

'What are you up to?' he said, angrily. 'I was watching that.'

Chris ignored the note of danger. She sniffed.

'Oh leave off, Dad,' she said. 'If you was that interested, why did you go out, then?'

He stood in front of the television, glowering.

'Are you going to switch it back or am I going to clip your ear?' he said.

'Oh grow up,' she said. 'You switch the bleeding thing back if you want it that much. You're standing next to it.'

Her father sprang at her and knocked her off her chair. Christine, sprawled on the floor, looked up at him. She was not angry, just utterly fed up.

'You stupid old git,' she said. 'Why don't you stop chucking your weight about? You bloody Sawdust Samson.'

Mrs Spalding had entered the room with the tray of tea things. She sided with her daughter.

'Ted,' she said. 'For Christ's sake what are you playing at? You can't go hitting Chris like that.'

It was said almost mildly, but it seemed to be the last straw. A hand shot out, the tray went flying, cups were smashed. The teapot too, and Mrs Spalding shrieked as a gush of boiling liquid stained the wallpaper brown. For a few minutes there was a free-for-all, and in the middle of it, over the bangs and shouting, Sharon woke up upstairs and began to shriek the place down. It was bedlam. Christine, her face stinging from a clout, escaped from the melee and dashed to her room. She dragged Sharon from her cot and lay down on the bed with her. For five minutes they cried in unison, and Christine babbled at her daughter. Oh hell, she said, Oh hell oh hell oh hell. They're mad, Sharon, this is a bloody madhouse and you're all I've got. I love you, Sharon, I love you, I love you, I love you. Then she listened to the noise from downstairs, where her parents appeared to be beating the living daylights out of each other. All over her and her pissy little baby. All it needed now, she thought, was for Sally Gerrold to turn up. That would just about finish it. That would be the end.

Sally did not turn up, though, and the end of the evening was even odder than its start. For Christine, absorbed at last in getting Sharon back to sleep, gradually became aware that the noises from downstairs had changed. Sharon was almost out, just making the occasional gooing noise, so Christine was able to concentrate. She could not believe it for a time, but it was true, there was no mistaking it. They were laughing! She put her baby in its cot and opened the bedroom door to listen better. There were gales of laughter, sobs of it. She bounded downstairs and threw open the living room door.

The scene was chaos. Two chairs were on their sides, the sideboard had been swept clean, there were shards of china everywhere. And on Mum's best patterned carpet there was

31

a gooey mix of tea, and milk, and sandwiches. With a sprinkling of crisps. In the middle of it, face to face and with their heads touching as they swayed forward, were Mum and Dad. Almost wetting themselves. It was infectious, and she very soon joined in, although she had not a notion what they found so funny. When they'd laughed themselves to a standstill they found another teapot and had a cup of tea, then cleared up the mess together. When they went to bed at last, Dad kissed her goodnight with a real hard hug.

He hadn't done that for ages.

Like the fool that she was, Christine told Sally about the fight. She had no need to, but she felt happier than she had for a long time, and it had all ended up so well, and anyway, it was a funny story.

It had ended up well because the next day, after all the laughter and a good night's sleep, she and her dad and mum had had a long talk about things and cleared the air. She'd told them how bored she got, and how she felt shut in, and trapped and so on, and her father admitted that he still felt bad about what she'd done sometimes, and what people thought behind their backs, and how he – foolishly – expected her to behave less like a teenager of sixteen and more like a grown-up now she'd got the baby – even if that meant watching boring TV stuff instead of listening to her trannie all the time. They agreed that she needed to get out more, and to meet more people of her own age, and to be free of Sharon occasionally, just once in a while.

Although it wasn't spelled out then, the implication was that Dad was going to ease up on his rule about Mum helping with the baby. And he suggested – he suggested it himself – that she should perhaps think about going out in the evening sometimes, with her friends. Christine realised what an act of trust this was, for Dad, because she knew how

32

shattered he had been by everything, how appalled he'd been by what she'd done. She said she'd think it over, and she thanked them over and over again. The row had turned out great, they all agreed. Crazy, wasn't it?

Two days later Christine spent the afternoon, alone, cruising round the shops. It was like being reborn, not having Sharon with her, and it turned out like a Christmas shopping spree. She bought her mum a daft new teapot – shaped like a purple elephant complete with a turbanned boy as the handle on the lid – for £11 from an antique shop, and then bought her dad a lovely cardigan. She went to the coffee bar where she guessed her mates would be, and met Mandy and Claire and Sophie, with Steven and Tim. Unlike the other times, she felt relaxed with everyone, now she didn't have a baby to tote around, and they nattered on for ages. When she went home she took a four-pack of Guinness for her dad, a bottle of sweet sherry for her mum, and a bottle of Martini Rosso to keep in her room. After she'd given out the presents, and had tea, and bathed the baby and put her to bed, she settled down to have a read and listen to the radio. She'd had some sherry downstairs, and she opened the Rosso and poured a half a tumbler onto some ice she'd brought up from the fridge. She was happy.

When Sally Gerrold arrived she noticed it at once, and asked what was going on. Christine laughed, and said she'd had a row with Mum and Dad, and made it up, and they'd been celebrating. She offered Sally a drink, and Sally said no thank you, so Christine poured herself another big one and swirled the ice around. Then she told Sally all about the fight, and what a great laugh it had been. She added a fair number of extra touches of her own, in fact, to make it more spectacular. The television had been knocked for a loop, she said, and all the china in the house was smashed, and the neighbours had been hammering on the walls – it had been hilarious. She offered the bottle again, it was once more declined, and she poured another tot into her glass.

'You're not drunk are you, Christine?' asked Sally Gerrold.

'Of course I'm not!' said Chris. 'Just merry, that's all. We all need to have a little drink now and then, don't we?'

'Mm,' went Sally Gerrold.

'I've always reckoned dipping a baby's dummy in Guinness is a good plan,' Christine rattled on. 'That's what I'll do when our Sharon needs it. That's what my Mum did to me. Go on, have a drink, love.'

'I hate to see a dummy in a baby's mouth,' said Sally, waving away the bottle. 'Won't it be nice when she gets older and doesn't need one? Well, she doesn't really need one now. It won't be long before she'll do without.'

'Do without?' said Christine. 'That's daft. It keeps the little bugger quiet, doesn't it?'

'Yes, but it does look rather awful, doesn't it? When a baby's older. I hate to see it, don't you?'

Christine didn't, but she wasn't drunk enough to say so. She shut up, rather obviously. Sally looked at her watch.

'Look, I'd better shift,' she said. 'You don't need me tonight, that's for sure. I'll leave you to your . . . party.'

'All right,' said Christine. 'See you then. Thanks for dropping in. Are you sure you won't have a little drink? It's good stuff, this, dead spicy.'

'No, I won't thanks,' said Sally, collecting up her gear. 'And Christine – you won't drink *too* much, will you?'

Christine giggled.

'Course I won't,' she said. 'Don't *worry*, Sally love. It's just a celebration, that's all. I just feel good, all right?'

Sally gave her a smile, although not much of one, and left. When she'd gone, Chris stared at the door for a moment or two.

'Christ Almighty, Sal,' she said, half under her breath. 'You can't half be straight at times. Don't you *ever* let things go?'

It was not for another three weeks that Christine decided to test out her father's babysitting offer, and she started with a real hard test. She was invited to a party by Claire, who rang up on a Friday afternoon. Claire, like most of her mates, was still without a job, and she said they were all getting frantic. Anytime anyone could get a place free, she said, they got together for a bash, just to keep from going mad. All the old crowd would be there, and if Chris could get a bottle, great; none of them had a lot of cash to chuck around.

The party was for the Saturday night, and Christine asked her mum and dad later that Friday evening, after Sharon had been put to bed. She'd spent ages wondering how to drop it tactfully, or make it sound like an old-girls' school reunion, but she'd got nowhere. In the end, over a cup of tea, she'd just said as casually as she could that Claire had rung her up that afternoon.

They both knew Claire, but they both knew Christine. Something in her voice made it perfectly plain that things were afoot. They waited.

'There's a party on at her place tomorrow night, that's all,' she said. 'Her mum's place. She asked me if I'd like to go, that's all.'

Her father's face said 'No!' immediately. But her mother wasn't having that.

'Well, we did say, Ted,' she told him, in a soothing voice. 'Any time you want an evening out, we said. After the teapot row. We can't just go back on it, you know, not just like that. What's your objection?'

Very daring, Christine thought. Her dad's objection was only too clear. Apart from anything else, she'd told her parents – untruthfully as it happened – that she'd got

35

pregnant after getting plastered at a party. Here we go again, he must have thought.

'I won't stay late,' she said. 'I just want a break, that's all. All my friends'll be there. I'll be able to catch up on the gossip, have a chat. I promise I won't stay late.'

'What's late?' said her father, aggressively. 'Two o'clock in the morning's not late, is it? It's the early hours. Three o'clock. Four o'clock. Be back in time for an early breakfast. That's not late.'

'Ted,' said her mother. 'Come on now, love. You did say. You can't go back on it.'

Christine did a calculation in her mind. When it would start to get lively enough to bother with. How she could get back. She split it down the middle.

'I could be back by midnight, Dad,' she said. She tried a joke. 'Before the bus turns into a pumpkin and three white mice.'

'Ten o'clock,' he said. 'That's final. Be back by ten o'clock and you can go.'

'Don't be so bloody silly!' said Mrs Spalding. 'Ten o'clock! Don't be so bloody wet!'

Christine let them fight it out between them. She didn't mind a lot what time they wanted her back, it was the principle that mattered. The thought of getting out at all was wonderful, and her old man would soon ease up on details when he saw she could be trusted. And she could, she knew it, not a doubt in the whole wide world. But she'd grown up enough, in the last year or so, to recognise her father's fears. And respect them. She let the argument – which was friendly anyway – roll on.

In the end they settled on eleven, with her father waiting opposite the house to pick her up. Although that did not suit her half so well (there was something demeaning about being picked up, something her mates would never understand, would mock at) she agreed. She thanked her father meekly, and told him she was grateful. He looked hard at her, to see if there was satire in her face, but there was not, not the slightest trace. He softened.

'Sorry to be such a killjoy, Chris,' he said. 'But I'll get over it. Give us a little bit of time, eh? I'll get over it.'

As parties went it was all right, although not the greatest in the history of the world by any means. But Chris enjoyed herself immensely. She did not dance, because she did not want to, but she found she was no longer jumpy every time a boy suggested it, or looked at her in that certain way. She spent most of the time in the kitchen with a drifting crowd of girls and the occasional boy, drinking sweet cider and yapping. There was a fair amount of scandal about people in her set, although not much of it was sexual. Lots more of them had paired off, and Sue and Andrew had actually got married. But she remained, to everyone's amazement, the only one who'd got in pod. Maybe she was unnatural!

On the dot of eleven, without telling anyone she was being met, she did her Cinderella act, using Sharon's feeding time as her excuse. Her father tried to be jovial and relaxed on the drive home, but he still hadn't come to terms with it all. But Christine was demure, and had sucked a mint-sweet to take the cider off her breath, and said it had been all right, if a little quiet. Her father snorted, because he'd been sitting in the car outside for fifteen minutes and had watched the teenage loonies (as he thought them) going in, and heard the ear-shatteringly loud (as he thought it) music coming out. But he didn't argue.

Christine left it for nearly a fortnight after that, then she went out for the evening with Sophie and Mandy, just to sit at Sophie's house and play records and talk. Tim, who was going out with Mandy now, turned up at about nine, and suggested they all went down the Pineapple for a drink, but they declined. They knew that Christine was on probation, so to speak, and they did not want to put her on the spot.

37

This time her dad let her make her own way home, by bus, and she got there twenty minutes before the half past ten deadline. The following week she went out twice, and was in by 10.30 on the dot, and the week after that she went to another party. Not only did her father extend her home-time till twelve o'clock, but he didn't pick her up. She liked that.

Although she never thought out why, Christine never told Sally Gerrold about these jaunts. And although she didn't ask them not to, neither did her parents. It was crazy, but it was a sort of guilty secret between the three of them. Christine had never told them what Sally had said about babysitting – even *them* babysitting – but they seemed to have picked up the signals somehow. So when Sally called, and the subject of evening boredom came up as it occasionally did, Christine made a face and acted as though she still spent all her nights at home, except on family visits with the baby.

The disaster happened suddenly, and it shattered everything. Christine went out to a party, a long way out, and someone spiked the punch. She got drunk, but not outrageously, and she got let down. The girl who said her boyfriend would drive them home by one o'clock – Christine's specially-negotiated deadline for this one special party – got ten times worse than Christine, and threw up over her bloke. He disappeared in a rage, leaving his girlfriend spewing and screaming hysterically, and of course, he did not come back. Another boy tried half-heartedly to drag Christine into a bedroom, and it started a fight in which her dress was torn half off and she got a bruised eye. She tried to phone a taxi but the radio-girl, listening to the music and the mayhem down the phone, put out a general call for all her drivers to *avoid* the address, not go there, it was the usual thing. Christine, woozy, weepy and desperate, set off to walk, minus one shoe when she started, both when she got home. It was just after three a.m.

Christine's father had his coat on and his car keys in his hand. His face was white with rage, and his cheek was scratched. Mrs Spalding was crouching in an armchair, halfway between fury and tears. Once again Sharon was crying, and once again the furniture was disarranged. This time, though, there was not a hint of laughter, nor any possibility that it would come. It would be the police this time, more like, thought Christine, as her father dragged her through the door and screeched at her. Already next door's bedroom light was on. If they weren't careful, it would soon be the whole street.

It wasn't a shouting match, though, after the first few seconds. Mr Spalding looked at the state of Christine's dress, and her torn tights, and a look of loathing contorted his face. He spat onto the floor in front of her, actually onto the carpet.

'You dirty little whore,' he said. 'You fill me with disgust.'

Christine was drunk, almost too drunk to care, certainly too drunk to try to tell her story. She tried to pass her father, who jumped back as if she had the plague. She staggered past and went up to her bed. Sharon was screaming, still, and she slapped her across the face, as hard as she could within the confines of the cot. Then she was sick. Then she cleaned up the baby, and the floor, and gave her a bottle and took her into bed, and they both went to sleep.

This time, there was not any laughter down below.

This time, also, there was no getting over it, no clearing of the air because of the bust-up. When Christine came downstairs next morning her father had gone out, a thing he rarely did on Sunday, and her mother was like ice. For hours she would not even talk to Christine, let alone talk about what had happened, and Christine, hungover and resentful, began to get as stubborn as her mother. That evening she refused to eat with her – like Dad, who had already refused to eat with *them* – and she did not even answer when her mother tried to make a gesture, said miserably: 'Look Chris, we've got to have this out, we've got to talk, it's useless going on like this.'

Next day, when her father was at work, she did speak to her mother, but they were both very edgy and reserved. Chris had long ago abandoned any idea of saying she was sorry, because she thought their attitude was so untrusting, so disgusting, that they'd forfeited any right to it. In any case, the whole incident had dwindled in her mind to what it really was: no big deal, the sort of thing that happened all the time at parties. Anyone would think she'd been selling herself to sailors for fifty p. the way her mother looked at her. She couldn't be bothered with it. She couldn't even be bothered to say what had happened, to deny the unspoken accusations.

'If he wants to behave like a stupid, sulky kid,' she told her mother, 'that's his lookout. And yours too. You can bloody believe what you like.'

She knew she was being stupid, and ridiculous, and unfair, but that was that. She knew what a vast act of trust her father had forced himself into, and she knew that if she grovelled for a while, until he'd listen, then told him the plain, unvarnished truth, he'd see reason, and probably be ashamed into the bargain. But sod it, why should she? Two could play at silly-buggers. Two could play at cutting off their nose to spite their face. She let him stew for a while. They could all suffer.

It was an awful strain though, because the longer it went on, the worse it got. The sheer iciness of her father's hostility was a continual shock to her, and she realised very quickly that it was running out of control. If she wanted to make it up now, she'd probably left it too late; any point of contact, any way of getting the subject sensibly brought up, was receding rapidly. If she sat at table with them – which she did less frequently – it was awful. The tension and dislike was almost palpable, it was horrendous. And her mother started cracking with the strain, and she directed her fear and anger at her daughter. For the first time that Christine could remember, her mother took her father's side against her. She began to treat her like a stranger, and a dirty one at that. Things were getting dreadful, fast. They were running out of control.

The first time Sally Gerrold called after the bust-up, Christine had denied that it was serious, and had not told the social worker what it was about. How could she, after all? Sally did not know she had been going out at night, and had stated quite specifically what she had thought of the babysitter lark. She must have suspected something big had happened, because of the state she found Chris in, but she was left whistling for an explanation. But the second time she visited, Christine was already in tears when she arrived. And she confessed.

If Sally was surprised to hear that Christine had been to pubs and parties, had been meeting her old friends at night and having a good time, she did not let it show. Not that Chris would have noticed, probably, because she was in constant floods of tears and she had a hankie clutched to her nose and eyes most of the time, to avoid having to look at Sally's face. She did want to know exactly what had gone on at the last party, however, and she questioned Christine closely, as if she didn't quite believe that nothing else had happened.

"But if you're *sure* that's all there was,' she said. 'If you *insist* that you didn't have sex or anything, what is there to worry about?'

Even in her misery Christine felt rather outraged.

'Sure?' she said. 'Of course I'm bloody sure, aren't I? I

41

wouldn't have sex any more if it was my last day on earth. This berk that tried to rape me almost got his face filled in.'

'Rape you?' said Sally. 'Did someone try to rape you?'

There were only two ways to go. Christine could either explode or she could cool it. She cooled it. She felt incredibly depressed.

'No one tried to rape me, Sal,' she said. 'It was just a lark or something, I don't know. The point is I didn't want it. I don't want nothing like that. All I wanted was to get home to me dad, like I'd promised. And now he won't speak to me. It's terrible.'

'But why don't you tell him, then?' asked Sally. Christine almost screamed.

'Because I can't. Because he won't stay in the room with me. Because he hates me. Because he thinks I'm just a cheap little tart who goes with anyone who wants to have me. That's why. That's why. That's why.'

She wouldn't talk any more. She wanted to go to bed, she said. Sally went downstairs to have a talk with Mr and Mrs Spalding. She told them what Christine had said, how it had all been a ghastly accident, and that nothing . . . untoward, improper . . . had taken place. Halfway through her speech Mr Spalding got up from his chair unceremoniously and walked out. Mrs Spalding, tight-lipped, told Sally that she was wasting her time on her daughter. She was a selfish, immature little madam, she said, who didn't deserve a father like she had. She was a selfish, sluttish little bitch.

Being a slut was one thing nobody could ever accuse Christine Spalding of, Sally thought. But over the next few weeks, on her much more frequent visits, she noticed a remarkable change in her. Christine went into a decline, a rapid one, that seemed to spiral. First her room got untidy, then messy, then dirty. Then the baby followed on the same drab course. Her glowing white woollies grew grubby, then greyish. Every time Sally called, Christine was sunk in gloom. The room began to smell.

One afternoon, Christine was crying when Sally Gerrold turned up. She met Mrs Spalding on the stairs and Mrs Spalding was angry.

'She'll have to pull herself together,' she said. 'It's disgusting. That poor little baby's suffering now. It needs changing and she won't change it, and she won't let me in her room. You'll have to sort her out, Miss Gerrold. You'll have to sort her out before my husband *chucks* her out. There!'

In the bedroom, Chris was sitting on the bed. Her shoulders were hunched and tears were running down her face. Little Sharon was crawling round the floor, a full nappy hanging from her bottom, leaking onto the carpet. The place was getting like a tip.

Sally Gerrold, as a social worker, was used to many things. She got the changing-mat cleaned up, she boiled up some water, she sorted out a nappy and some cream. While Christine sat there sniffing, she stripped the baby, cleaned up the mess, then washed her, rubbed in cream and pinned a nappy on. She did not do it very expertly, but Christine made no move to help, she showed no interest. Sally made up a bottle, and put Sharon in her cot. Then she made them both a coffee and sat beside Chris on the bed.

'Cheer up,' she said. 'While there's life there's hope.'

After a while, Christine began a monologue. Everything was hopeless, she said, she just couldn't go on any more. Dad hated her, she hated Dad, Mum hated them both. She'd have to run away. She'd have to kill herself. She'd have to kill the baby. Suicide, murder, despair. She couldn't get up in the mornings, she couldn't be bothered to take her clothes off at night, she was going insane. She was trapped in the house, she was trapped in the room, she was trapped by her

43

life. Everything was deteriorating, her dad had gone mad, she couldn't take much more. Look at that bloody baby, Sal, she said. Look at it there, smiling and gurgling like a lunatic. I give it everything and what does it do? It shits on me best jeans. I hate it sometimes, Sally. I really do.

Sally smiled.

'Well, you know what I always say, Chris,' she said. 'It's all unnatural anyway, this motherhood stuff. All conditioning.'

She was being falsely jovial, but Christine was too depressed and self-absorbed to answer, let alone to take it seriously. The next words did sink in, though. Very far and very fast. They snapped her right back to reality, the here and now.

'Listen,' said Sally Gerrold. 'I've been thinking very seriously. Why not let Sharon go into care for a while? Just for a break. I—'

Christine was on her feet like a shot.

'No!' she said. 'Sharon stays with me! You can't take my baby away!'

'Sit down, Chris, do,' said Sally. 'No one's taking anyone away. I'm talking about a voluntary break, that's all. A short time for you to get adjusted. A little gap in the responsibility so that you can get it together with your mum and dad. You're in a mess, Chris, all of you. You're all in a truly dreadful state.'

Christine sat down and Sally let her cry. She explained, as the tears flowed, that it was completely voluntary, that Sharon would be looked after in someone's house, it wouldn't be in a home or anything like that. No one was trying to separate them, she could visit as much as she liked 'until things were sorted out'. Sharon would be out of everybody's hair and they could patch the family up again, get things back to normal. She'd thought it out herself, and all she asked of Christine was that she did the same. Just think about it, nothing more, all right?

In bed, that night, Christine did. At first she rejected it, completely. But later on, she heard her parents rowing down below, as they did so often these days, and always over her, no question. Then later still Sharon woke up screaming, and she almost lay there and let her scream. When she got up to attend to her she felt old, and worn out, and finished. And that was stupid, at the age of sixteen, let's face it. As she cleaned her daughter up she thought of a few days break. A dance or two, a drink with her friends, a concert at the Apollo maybe. And Sharon well looked after. She would be. She would be.

She sat on the bed, with Sharon lying on her nappy waiting to be pinned, thinking she would do it. What a funny girl that Sally could be, though, she thought. All that crap about motherhood being unnatural, and conditioning. She laughed. All that crap! She turned her daughter over, lovingly, and kissed her little bum. She felt a great weight lifted.

If things had got any better with her parents, Christine would have reconsidered. But the next two days were absolutely awful. On the third day, after more explanations and exhortations from Sally, after sleepless hours of worry and misery, after thinking she understood the implications, then being sure she did not, she signed some forms. Convinced, finally, of what? That she did not know for certain any more what she thought, or felt, or knew – except she trusted Sally. Completely. Well she had to, didn't she? They left the house together – furtively – and took Sharon to the Social Services department at Ringwood House in Sally's green mini. There, with a heavy heart and a peculiar parallel feeling of relief, Christine kissed Sharon goodbye. For a while. A short while only.

She cried on Sally's shoulder afterwards, and told her,

brokenly, that she was her friend, her only friend. Sally smiled.

'I hope so, Chris,' she said. 'I'm doing it out of friendship, truly. I think I'm doing my best for you. For everyone.'

They had a cup of coffee and a cake.

TWO

THE BLOW FELL one week later to the day, and it came in a pale-brown, innocent envelope. It came at the end of a week in which Christine had been almost happy, at the end of a week in which she and her parents had faced up to their problems, looked into the pit before them, and moved back, shaken. She tore open the envelope at breakfast time and took out the letter. Her father had already gone to work.

It was not a letter, exactly, it was a memo. It stated this:

> To: Miss Christine Spalding.
> From: The Director of Social Services.
> I hereby give you notice on behalf of the City Council that a resolution has been passed in accordance with Section 3 of the Child Care Act, 1980, that in the best interests of your child the said council should assume parental rights and duties on the grounds that you are of such habits and modes of life as to be unfit to have the care of the child. This means that your powers and duties in respect of Sharon Spalding are now vested in the council until she attains the age of 18, and that you will not be permitted to visit the child, or take her out

46

of the council's care, unless you are given permission so to do. If you should object to this resolution you may write to me within one month stating your objection. Within fourteen days of any objection so received the City Council may refer the matter to a Juvenile Court, where the Justices would decide whether parental rights or duties should rest with you or with the council.

Christine's mother was in the front room when Christine read the memo, and she returned when she heard the crash of breaking crockery. Christine was standing beside the table, holding the back of her chair, and her cup and the milk jug were on the floor. She was bone-white and shaking, holding her breath like a child in a crying fit, unable to speak. Her mother looked at her, terrified, then took the memo. She read it and they stared at each other, now equally white.

'They've taken her away,' Chris whispered. 'They've taken away my baby. Oh my God. Oh my God, Mum. I don't believe it.'

When Christine had told her parents seven days before that she had given Sharon – voluntarily – into temporary care, she had been terrified at how they might react. It seemed to her, and presumably to Sally Gerrold also, that their relationship was ruined, in tatters, destroyed beyond repair. But their reaction had been extraordinary. They did not ask her reasons, they did not shout, they did not scream. What's more, and even better, they clearly weren't relieved, even secretly. They were horrified, brought up short, brought to a full stop. Her father had gone pale, and stood up from his armchair, and sat down again. He had tried to speak, failed, stood up once more. It had become alarmingly clear that he was close to bursting into tears. Christine had fled from the room.

47

When she had returned, ten minutes later, her parents were composed. Her father had spoken to her, made a speech almost, an oddly formal speech. He told her that he and her mother wished to apologise. That they had let her down. They were sorry, he said, utterly sorry. For what they had done to her. Again he came close to tears. They all came close to tears. But a strange happiness grew up between them. It was an odd, euphoric time.

She had told them on a wave of courage, desperation, when she could no longer hope to hide for very long the fact of Sharon's disappearance. She had stalked into the living room, ignored the grim atmosphere, and blurted out her story. Afterwards, they had sat down and talked, properly, for the first time in ages, about the future. Then, for the next few days, they had talked of little else.

It was suggested immediately, and agreed, that they should use the time of Sharon's voluntary absence to get themselves together, to sort themselves out. She would be away a short time, they also agreed – no more than ten days or a fortnight. And for that time, Christine was persuaded, it would be better if she left her quite alone, did not attempt to visit, did not even make enquiries. It would show she was serious, and Sally Gerrold would get in touch if anything went wrong, that was obvious. Better to have a break, a clean break, for a week or two. Christine argued, but she could see the sense of it. They'd got into a state, all of them. This time would heal. This short break would relieve the situation.

They worked at it with a will, and Christine crushed the longing to see and hold her daughter that gnawed constantly at her. She spring-cleaned her room, she talked over Dad's idea of converting the top of the house into a flat for her and Sharon, they fantasised about the future, the better times they had to come. They also went out on little drives, spent a night at the cinema, and sat and chatted easily at home. Apart from the ache, it was one of the best times for ages, and Christine appreciated it beyond words. Mandy rang her up one evening and invited her to a party. No, she said. Go on, said Mum and Dad, why don't you? No, she said. Perhaps some other time. She felt happy saying it, almost like their little girl again.

So when the blow fell, Christine almost caved in. In the hours, then the days and weeks that followed, she became confused, disoriented. Time, and many features of reality, became a mist. Things seemed to happen ultra fast, or ultra slowly, or in a dream. She often lost touch with what she was doing, what other people were doing, what was going on. Inside her was an empty hole, a void so cold and vast that at times she almost choked. At almost every point she could not comprehend that it was happening. That Sally Gerrold had done this to her. Sally Gerrold.

On the morning that the blow fell, Mrs Spalding recovered first. She sat Christine, white and silent, in front of the gas fire and turned it on to full. She made her another cup of tea and almost filled it to the brim with sugar. She looked at the clock above the cooker and went to the telephone, to phone her husband, to get him back. But he was not there. He had gone out to see a customer in a warehouse. Mrs Spalding left a message that he must come home immediately he returned. There had been a family crisis.

When Christine was calm enough to talk, Mrs Spalding tried to reassure her. She was not well-versed in legal things, or official matters, but she was no one's fool. She said there must have been some mistake, she insisted that nobody could get away with such a thing, she was certain that no law or regulation could be so cruel. 'We'll get a solicitor, love,' she said, over and over. 'Your dad will know. We'll fight it all the way. We'll get a solicitor. But first we'll phone. Dry your eyes, my darling, then we'll phone them up.

There's been a mistake, that's all. It's just some awful mistake.'

Christine, staring into her cup, shivering in spite of the gas-fire's blast, could only mumble. She had the memo on her lap, she kept picking at it, touching it as if to make it disappear.

'But what do they mean?' she said. 'Mum, what can they possibly mean? "Such habits and modes of life as to be unfit." Unfit! Me! To bring up little Sharon. Oh Mum. Oh Mum. Oh Mum. I'm her bloody *mother*, Mum. What can they possibly mean?'

She rang at last, with her mother at her side, the number on the bottom of the memo. She spoke so quietly that the switchboard girl at Ringwood House had to ask her to speak up three times. She asked for Sally Gerrold.

There was a click, and a girl's voice answered. 'Sally,' said Christine, her voice wobbling. 'It's me, Christine.'

There was another click, then a girl's voice once more. The same one? Sally Gerrold was not there, in any case, that was the message Christine got. She was out of the office. When would she be back? Ah. Nobody was quite sure. Could they get her to call? Well, would she know the number? I'll ring back, said Christine, hopelessly. She fell onto her knees beside the phone, and hugged her mother's legs.

Over the next two hours, Christine rang six more times, and her mother twice. Christine became more and more obsessed by the conviction that Sally Gerrold was indeed in Ringwood House, and was determined not to speak to her. She was brushed off less and less politely, and she became less and less coherent. She had become light-headed, anyway, because her mother kept making her cups of tea, and she had sicked up all her breakfast. Her mother was also getting frantic, afraid for Christine's state, her sanity almost. She rang her husband's firm three times but he had not come back, he had not rung his office and they could not get in contact, there was no 'machinery'.

In the end a man's voice spoke to Christine very sternly. She shouted hysterically at him once or twice, and he silenced her with the harshness and the coldness of his tone. She tried to interrupt, she whimpered, but he crushed her with authority. He advised her not to issue threats, he advised her not to act so childishly. Whatever had been done, he said, had been done for the good of all concerned, and had been a decision taken by professionals, by experts. Whatever Miss Sally Gerrold had decided would have been the result of long and careful observation, for the best reasons and the best motives. Her recommendations would have been scrutinised by senior officers and ratified by the experienced councillors of the Social Services Committee. I repeat, he said, whatever has been done has been done for the good of all concerned.

Christine said: 'But there's only two concerned. Me and my baby. There's only two concerned.'

The man's voice began, but Christine cut it off.

'You bastard!' she shrieked. 'You fucking heartless bastard!'

After a silence he resumed. His voice was not angry; smooth, rather. He said:

'We do not make these decisions lightly, you know. And I am deeply angered by your assumption that we do. I am also deeply angered by your disgraceful behaviour, which can only lead me to the conclusion that this was an utterly right decision. The interests of the child, the interests of the child alone, are paramount. A child, in this case, that you have not even seen fit to visit, or enquire after. Since you gave it *voluntarily* into care. That, in itself, speaks volumes.'

Who hung up then, Christine did not know. She hardly knew what happened next. Her father did not get in touch, her mother tried to stop her going out, or going mad,

51

whatever. The next thing Christine knew for certain was that she was near to Ringwood House and she was drunk. Not very, surely, for she had bought a bottle of Martini Rosso and swigged from it only four times or so, before it had slipped into the gutter and broken. She had enough control of her mind and fingers to go into a phone box near to Ringwood House and make a call, although it did take her a more than usual time to press the money into the slot. She knew that Sally Gerrold was in her office this time, for certain. Because her car was parked outside, in the car park. Her green mini. The traitor car.

But Sally Gerrold was not in, they said. Or she was busy, maybe. Could they take a message? Or would she like, again, to speak to the direc – Christine slammed the phone down. And when she'd slammed it down, she went to Sally Gerrold's car. She took a half a brick from a nearby builder's skip, and she slammed it down on Sally's car. On the roof. It made a lot of noise, but not much else. There was hardly a scratch. Christine banged again, then scraped it down the side. Still very little outward sign. As the doors of Ringwood House pushed open, and officials hurried out, Christine started bashing at the windscreen. She was weak, like a rag doll apparently, and the glass was amazingly tough, it would not break. She was exhausted, tired and enraged.

When Sally Gerrold came out, and ran towards her car, Christine got a short-lived lease of strength. With a sharp crack the windscreen turned to frost. The brick bounced to the ground, and Christine threw herself at Sally, her hands like claws, her teeth bared. As she bore her to the ground she was screeching.

'I want my baby. I want my baby. I want my baby,' she cried.

She was pulled roughly off the social worker, and restrained.

*   *   *

Everyone was marvellous, of course. The solicitor the Spaldings had engaged was almost moved by how marvellously generous the Social Services department had been, and Sally Gerrold most of all. She was quite prepared, he said, to let the matter rest, although a prosecution for criminal damage would have been the logical course, and the police, had they been called, would certainly have suggested a further summons, for assault. But if the family were prepared to pay for the windscreen, and for some minor scratches to be painted out, and for Sally Gerrold's outfit to be cleaned – well, there the matter would end. Most extremely generous, and compassionate, of all concerned.

But what of the rest, they said. (Or rather, Mr and Mrs Spalding said. Christine had by now retreated, had become withdrawn. She hardly talked, or ate, or looked at anyone. She was worse than she had ever been, far worse.) What of the loss of the baby, the appeal? What of the process – the mysterious, stark, terrifying process – by which the City Council had stolen their daughter's daughter?

The solicitor shook his head reprovingly, and deprecated such language. Nobody, he said with a smile, had 'stolen' anybody else. Whether or not one agreed that the course was necessary, or even desirable, it had all been done in the best of good faith. The removal of Sharon from her mother's care was no light thing, no snap decision. The people who had decided on the course, he said, were experts. They could be challenged on details, certainly; they might indeed prove to have come to a regrettable decision. But nobody could – or should – infer bad faith. They had acted in the way they had for reasons they thought good. A social worker had observed, her seniors had examined and ratified her assessments, the duly-elected members of the local authority had considered their recommendation. And endorsed it fully.

'But they're wrong,' said Mr Spalding, bitterly. 'They're

bloody wrong, can't you see that? That stuck-up, dozy, stupid little . . . What does she understand about . . . The . . .'

The eyes of the solicitor were on his face, and his wife's hand was on his sleeve. He shut his mouth. The solicitor nodded solemnly.

'If we are to win this case,' he said. 'We must all retain our self-control. Regrettably, Christine has already . . . Well, no more of that. My feeling now, is that we should not appeal.'

Even Christine was aroused. She lifted her chin from her chest and looked at him, with horrified eyes. Mr Spalding seemed about to explode. The solicitor raised his hand.

'Now listen, listen,' he went on. 'Let me finish. I'm not suggesting that we let the matter drop, not at all. But to appeal now, within the time suggested in the letter, would merely be foolhardy, a waste of energy. The damage to the car, the assault, Christine's rather . . . depressed . . . demeanour. It would be a waste of time, I promise you. We would fail. It is best to wait, I promise you. It is best to wait.'

The Spaldings, all three, exchanged glances. He was the expert, he was the law. They paid the money because he knew the ropes. He would be right, he had to be. More right than them, in any event. Christine mumbled despairingly: 'But they've got my baby girl. They won't even let me see her.'

When she had repeated it loudly enough for him to hear, the solicitor smiled a reassuring smile.

'I'm not an absolute expert in this field, my dear,' he said. 'But there I am sure you're wrong. I'm absolutely confident that you will be granted access. You will be able to visit Sharon, I can almost promise you.' Christine put her face in her hand. 'We'll let it all blow over,' he continued heartily. 'Then we'll see. I think we have to trust them to a great extent, to realise that they are acting for the best for little Sharon, as they see it. Trust them, and *do* trust me. Let it blow over, and we'll see what can be done. I am certain nothing will transpire which is wrong, or harmful, these laws have stood the test of time. And I am *certain* they will let you visit Sharon.'

The solicitor, as he had himself admitted, was not an absolute expert in the field. And on one essential point he was devastatingly, disastrously wrong in the advice he gave the Spaldings, and charged them for. But on the question of access – which for Christine was more immediately pressing than any other question in her life – he was right. She was informed by the department the very next morning that she could see her daughter. And for six weeks, on a Wednesday, she did just that.

Despite the fact that it cost him money – and if it went on for long enough would probably cost him his job – Christine's father drove her to the house in which Sharon was being fostered. Sally Gerrold, almost unbelievably to the Spaldings, was still the social worker on the case, and, naturally, Christine could hardly bear to think of her, let alone be driven in her car. She had received a letter from Sally in the week after things had all blown up, and she had been neither able to finish reading it, nor to keep it, which was foolish and regrettable. She had crumpled it, then torn it into tiny pieces in her rage. The letter had deplored her lack of maturity and gratitude (gratitude!) over a course of action that was necessary if the baby ('the baby') was to be enabled to grow up to lead a happy, normal and fulfilled life somewhat better structured and less damaged than her own. There were no reasons given in the letter, and Sally Gerrold's reasons were, in fact, never stated to the family. They were nothing to do with them. They were the mysteries of the profession, the province of the experts.

The foster parents, who had three children of their own, lived in a large semi-detached house about thirty five miles from the Spaldings. It had a big garden, with a stream at the bottom, and a field next door with horses in it. The first time Christine saw it, it struck terror into her soul. There were two cars in the drive, the children were beautifully dressed, the foster parents were smiling, relaxed, and friendly. Christine stood in front of them, white-faced, her eyes rimmed red and surrounded by dull, dark skin, and they offered her a glass of wine. They asked her – 'White or red?' Which did she prefer. . . ?

Christine and her father visited on six occasions – her father staying outside in the car except for two short peeks at Sharon – and all six occasions were appalling. The day before the visits Christine's state of mind got worse and worse, she sometimes cried uncontrollably for hours, far into the night, and she hardly ever slept, even with the sleeping pills her doctor had prescribed for her. On the mornings she was lifeless, catatonic practically, and unable to control the trembling in her hands. After each visit she was inconsolable, suicidal almost. Touching Sharon, holding her, was unbearable, torture. Then letting her go.

Sally Gerrold was in the house, tucked away in the kitchen with the foster parents. But the other children were not kept separate. They played around this pale and lifeless stranger who held their new little sister so awkwardly, trying to be friendly, but also curious at what she was doing there. One little boy, called Jeremy, was always asking questions. Sometimes Christine held Sharon so tightly that she feared she might crush her. Sometimes she thought she would, purposely. Crush her to death. Kill her. Murder her. It would be one way out.

On the sixth visit, Jeremy referred to Sharon as Chloe. And Christine, almost dropping the baby from her lap, grabbed him by the arm.

'What?' she said, her voice high. 'What did you say? What did you call my Sharon?'

Jeremy, being only six, did the sensible thing. He started screaming. He broke free and raced out of the room, squawking blue murder. The foster father and Sally Gerrold appeared like magic. The foster mother, presumably, was comforting her son.

Christine Spalding was upright, holding Sharon. But all the fight was gone. She asked what was going on, and Sally explained it quietly. Mr and Mrs Hollingsworth had decided to rename Sharon. They were going to call her Chloe, which was very nice, wasn't it? They were long-term foster parents who were, indeed, hoping to adopt one day. Everyone was sorry, though, that Christine had heard like that. It was regrettable, but Jerry was so young. Only six, of course. What could they do?

What could Christine do? She did not lose her temper, she did not pass out, she stood there gazing at them, stunned. Shortly afterwards she found herself in her father's car, going home. She could not talk about it for hours, but when she did, the Spaldings contacted their solicitor. After due investigation, he came to visit them, in person, an extraordinary thing in itself. But the solicitor, a humane and honest man, was prepared to face them, and admit a grave mistake. The original memo had given them four weeks in which to object. That four weeks was an absolute. He had advised them against appealing, and they were now too late. She had lost all rights to Sharon, all rights of any kind. The 1980 Act again.

'If we had appealed within the time, given the circumstances,' he said, 'we would have lost. Christine's actions, and her drinking, and her state of mind, would have made their case completely irrefutable. But by not appealing, as far as I can see, we have apparently lost all rights. It is iniquitous.'

57

'It's insane,' said Christine's father, flatly. 'But it doesn't surprise me any more. What can we do?'

The solicitor regarded him carefully.

'I don't know,' he said. 'This law is old – it goes back ages, not just 1980, that's evidence of tinkering, that date – and a lot of people have been trying to get it changed for quite some time. But governments don't like change, as such, they find it easier to make do and mend, to patch up, to fudge the issue, then they can't be blamed. There are guidelines to how it should be used these days, that theoretically mean the social services can't take advantage of confused, unhappy people any longer. If we could prove that the guidelines had not been followed, I'm sure we'd have a case.'

'What are they, then?' asked Christine Spalding's father. 'Did she do something wrong, that Sally Gerrold? Or did Chris . . .'

'Christine signed,' said the solicitor. 'The question really is her state of mind. Did she know what she was signing, did she understand completely, was it properly explained? Things like that.'

Christine's mother said: 'She can't remember why she signed. She can't even properly remember signing, she's told me. She was confu – She was conned.'

'I believe that now,' said the solicitor. 'A few weeks ago I would merely have winced at such a statement. I believe your daughter was . . . misused, and I fear that no one will admit it. We've got to try, though. We've got to try and determine exactly what was done, and how.'

'And *why*,' said Christine's mother. 'That's what I want to know. Why? Why? Why?'

The solicitor smiled, gravely.

'Unanswerable,' he said. 'But let's be realistic. Whatever we say, they, will riposte with things like this: Christine's behaviour was the cause. She was irrational, irresponsible, drank too much. The way she reacted to the later events as

58

well, like the changing of the baby's name, for instance; natural anguish and a mother's love won't wash with these people, or a court, I'm afraid. Mother's love and natural anguish are far too woolly and emotional to be taken seriously.'

Christine had said nothing. But at this, her eyes slowly filled. The solicitor saw, but went on talking.

'Once something like this has happened,' he said, 'once a mistake has been made, reversal is appallingly difficult. You will be looked upon – your daughter will be looked upon – as a feckless, reckless, immoral, evil person. Not a child in trouble any more, how could they admit it? They have self-righteousness on their side, it is their creed. Everybody is heartless and inadequate – can be – but them. It is their creed.'

He stopped. His smile had gone.

'I think this whole thing is shameful,' he said, 'and I will not let it drop. I will explore every avenue and challenge this decision all along the line. If we can prove they have flouted the guidelines, well and good, we have a case. If we cannot prove it – I will not give up. The matter shall not rest. And incidentally, Mr and Mrs Spalding, Christine: there will be no charge. From now on my services are free.'

Inappropriately, after this statement, he apologised once more, to the silent family. Then he left.

Three days later, a letter arrived from the Director of Social Services. It had been decided after careful considera-tion of her behaviour, and the best interests of the child known as Sharon Spalding, that her right of access should be withdrawn. It should be noted – in case of any rash action which might be contemplated – that the said child had been moved to different foster parents, at an address which would not be divulged. The social worker involved, Miss Sally Gerrold, had asked to be taken off the case in view of her inability to sustain a working relationship with her client in view of her client's irrational, unreasonable, and violent behaviour. Any further communications with the Social Services Department should, therefore, be addressed to the director at the above address. No attempt should be made to contact Miss Gerrold, or indeed, any other person but the said director.

So that was it. Christine Spalding, apparently, had no daughter. Christine Spalding had no rights.

It was some long time before Christine Spalding was capable of continuing the struggle, and it was the solicitor who had let her family down so badly who became the greatest help. He worked tirelessly and for nothing on their behalf, and he kept them going with encouragement when they considered giving up, just rotting in despair. He sought out, and put Christine in touch with, voluntary organisations who tried to fight such rulings, and with her MP, who also did his best.

There was one young woman in particular whom Christine liked to talk to. Although any feeling of friendship that may have grown, she crushed with loathing and contempt. She remembered Sally Gerrold all too well.

This woman was called June, and she worked for an outfit called Single Parents' Aid. She was youngish, only twenty eight, and she was full of humour, despite the misery of her work. She made Christine laugh a lot, which nobody else could do. At all. She told her not to try and find where Sharon was, and try and spy on her, because if she did she would be taken to yet more – and probably yet more distant – foster parents. It would be done for Sharon's own good, she said, even if it meant uprooting her from a warm and loving family. They would do it for the baby's good not once but many times – as many times as was necessary to keep Christine out. That baby, she said, was going to be made happy if it killed her! She made Christine laugh.

She told Christine of bizarre cases indeed – like a mother who was allowed to 'visit' her son but not to touch him. She could look at him, though – through a barred window. (It was, she explained seriously, very good for him, this child.) It was the way she said these things. Christine laughed.

But June was not always humourous. She could be very sober, very sad. She felt, she said, that many social workers would like to remove all children from backgrounds that did not match their own, and their personal prejudices, and truly could not see the medieval cruelty involved. But they were not monsters, she went on, although there were some who were stupid, and vindictive, that was inevitable. But Sally Gerrold say. It was June's guess that she found Christine's family, in their life together and their attitudes, chaotic, violent, incomprehensible. They were young, some social workers, inexperienced, and could not understand the differences: of class, of background. The different ways of loving and being loved.

'They want all children to grow up to be like them, Chris,' she said. 'They can't imagine that anyone could really *want* to bring up children any differently. If you like frozen chips and beefburgers and they like wholemeal bread and brie: you're finished. It's as simple as that, I sometimes think. As simple as that.'

She also told Christine not to hate them, not to condemn them all. They did a fantastic amount of good work, she said, for which they got hardly any praise. And if – under almost impossible circumstances – they made a decision that turned out to be wrong, like a battered baby say, or a dead one, they were treated in the Press as if they'd done the deed themselves. 'No-win situation, Chris,' said June. 'No-win situation.'

Christine was convinced. Although of exactly what, God alone knew, she did not. Although June could make her laugh, she cried a lot these days, spontaneously, hopelessly.

She was given to tears, these days. All she really wanted to know, was if, and how, she could get her baby back. How, she asked. How?

'Don't go mad,' said June, on one occasion. 'Don't run amuck. And don't give up hope.'

'But how much *should* I hope? That's what I want to know. How much hope is there? I want my baby, June. I want my Sharon back.'

Silence. June could not tell her how much hope there was, because she did not know. She did not say that there was much, or very little. She said nothing.

Christine wept. She was given to tears.

A Letter From Wally

DEAR MR WALKER,

I hope you don't mind me writing to you like this, out of the blue after all this time, but I'm out of my mind sitting here in Belfast, and I can't think of anyone else to write to. No, that sounds rude, and I don't mean it to. But in a daft sort of way you know more about me than anyone else, at least about this Army business, and in an even dafter sort of way I think I *ought* to write to you, you deserve it! In any case, I couldn't send a letter like this to my mum, now could I? She'd hardly be too chuffed to find her little sunshine had turned into a killer, even if she *did* want me to join. And in many ways this letter's a confession. I think you'll want to read it, I think you'll take it as a compliment. I think you'll understand.

First off, I'd better tell you who I am, though, because it's been some time. Wally Stimpson, special mate in your classes with Martin Holbrook, Tommy Jones and Bill Clayton. About five foot eight, straight black hair and a biggish nose, they used to call me Trunky. I know in the two years you had me you must have thought I was a right pain in the arse, and I was, I'm sorry. That's another reason why I'm writing, though.

The thing is, see, that although you never realised it – and you may find it hard to credit – I was always knocked out by your guts. Even when I was mocking with the others, taking the piss something merciless, I was amazed by you. I can say it in a letter – you were a little tubby wanker with pebble specs, and you were a lefty swine to boot. But you weren't afraid of us. I can still see you, standing there in front of twenty five big louts, all shouting and bawling, and you didn't give a bugger for any of us. You told us we were stupid, and ignorant, and horrible, and you told us why. That time you chucked out Martin and Bill, I wonder if you remember it? They gave you some old crap they'd worked out about how the Paks and Nignogs were taking all our jobs away, and you hit them with statistics until they looked dead stupid. And then you chucked them out because they wouldn't have it. They were stunned. They were going to beat you up.

Oh yes, Mr Walker, there were several plans to follow you home one dark night and fill you in, I bet that never occurred to you, did it? The closest you ever came was over the Army thing, when some of us decided to go in and you made those jokes about Joining the Professionals. The professional whats, you said. The professional corpses? The professional murderers? The professional bumlickers? Martin Holbrook was going to put a stocking on his head that night and smash your teeth and glasses in, but he didn't have the guts. D'you remember what you told him, when he said it would be better than the dole? You said: 'Oh come on Holbrook,' you said. 'Up to your neck in mud and bullets, no crumpet and compulsory washing. That can't be *really* better than the dole, can it?' Something like that. And he could only stare at you, like a pig's head on a slab. And hate you.

Funny, writing in this Irish barrack room, how clearly I can bring it back to mind, them college days. I can even see the colour of your shirt, when you told me not to join. You had me in your room, on a Wednesday afternoon, it was, and you told me that I'd never do it, you said I wasn't dim enough. *I* hated you for that, because I couldn't tell if you were being serious. If you were taking the piss. And you wouldn't tell me, either, you just laughed. I'd have listened to your arguments, I wanted to. But you just laughed at me. I suppose it served me right.

It's a Wednesday afternoon today, as it happens, and I've been sitting in these barracks for nearly four days and never been outside. The sun's shining, despite the time of year, and you can hear the traffic, and the kids playing in the school playground down the road. Some of the mob reckon it's deliberate, that, having a school so close. It might deter the mad Micks from having a go at us. I don't know any more, I've given up trying to think since Margaret Mary Byrne got killed. Eleven years old. All I can think, these days, is that the whole thing's hopeless, and I'm part of it. I joined.

Looking at what I've written, I've got another confession to make. Although I'm going to tell you all this, I don't know if you'll ever get it. I'm going to write it down all right, I've got to. But in the end, I probably won't send it. If I did, see, it wouldn't get out. It'd be intercepted, it would have to be. Not that our letters are censored, or anything like that, ho ho. But if I put this in an envelope and tried to send it out, I'd end up court-martialled. All right then. Here we go.

The daft thing is, Mr W, that even when I did join up, even when I walked out of your office thinking you were a prat, I half agreed with you. But when I looked into it, when I worked it out, I realised you were all to cock, you'd got it wrong. You were thinking of a different century. For a start-off – standards. They're incredible. I only just scraped through, and Holbrook and Clayton – no chance. There's even a *waiting* list for Christ's sake, since unemployment got so high. And from the word go, they confirmed what I'd worked out myself. If you played your cards right, you'd get more out than you put in. You'd see the world, you'd get a trade, you'd get experience. I reckoned then – and I still reckon now – that your chances of getting killed are pretty low, even in Northern Ireland, and the Falklands was a one-off, obviously. As for the nuclear bit – well, same difference. You can't go up any quicker when the big bang comes just because you wear a uniform, can you? You can be incinerated just as fast standing in front of a class of thickarses in a college of further education!

To be fair, I'd say all round I wasn't that far off the beam. I'd say the Army was a mixture, and I'd say it was a mixture that someone like you could never understand. Compared with what *I* had outside it was all right, more than all right in many ways. Compared with what a lot of them had outside it was fantastic. You'd probably reckon it was dreadful, and mindless, and sick, but people like you, Mr Walker, just don't know you're born. Because this is a confession, though, I've got to tell you this: it was not as bad as I expected, and it was a thousand times worse. Unluckily for me, the longer I've been in, the worse it's got. I've met a few others, too, quite a few, who are desperate. Sometimes we don't know where it will end. Sometimes, for some people, the end arrives. Margaret Mary Byrne.

The way they treat you during basic training suits most kids fine. It did me, certainly, it's been tried and tested, tested over years, decades. It's a combination of physical exhaustion, and fear of punishment, and some sort of half-religious thing about the regiment, and 'comradeship' and 'manhood'. Stupid from hindsight maybe; but whatever *you* might think, it's also lots of fun. It's great to be given a gun, and taught to fire it, and to be allowed to roar around in a five-ton truck or have a bash inside a tank. It's like toyland to most blokes of seventeen. It was to me.

There's more, of course. Psychology. Although they knacker you all day, they make ruddy sure you can go bananas in the evenings. The booze you go through is incredible, and if you show me a soldier who says he doesn't smoke, I'll show you a bloody liar. In a subtle kind of way they encourage you. The corporals and the lance-jacks take the young ones under their wing to show them the ropes, and mark their cards and so on. They get you into trouble, then – usually – get you out again. It's all part of the comrades bit, standing up for your mates. 'A' platoon can't have a drink with 'B' platoon unless it's like a competition. And if 'B' platoon appears to be winning – there'll be a punch-up. Stands to reason.

Going round in a team like this, and being expected to keep your end up all the time, leads to some pretty rare nights out, I can tell you. And you also find that people – especially in a garrison town – are a lot more tolerant than they would be if you were in a football crowd, or just a gang of hooligans. As long as you don't go mad and kill somebody, or rape too many women so to speak, you'll be all right. If a pub gets broken up you'll probably get a bollocking back at camp, and you might have to cough up some cash, the lot of you, to pay the damage. But it's all done on the nod. The landlord doesn't call the law, he calls liaison. 'Cause apart from anything else, you're his custom, aren't you? The jam on the bread. His next year's holidays in Majorca. Logic. It was after one of these great nights out, in fact, that I began to suss out some of what was going on.

I was based in a little dump not far from Winchester at the time, and my particular mates were called – oh what the hell, that's nothing to do with it. There was seven of us, anyway, and we'd gone out on the Friday night. It was a sleepy hole, and the dances were like necrophilia – dead boring! – so we'd all got tanked up pretty good before we went. Most of us also had a little half of something on the hip, to liven up the watered-down rubbish they sold us at the hall. It was the usual thing, you know: you spent most of the evening either insulting blokes in the hope of starting a bundle, or trying to grab lumps of female flesh as it danced past. I suppose I must have had a couple of proper dances, and the formula was, at the end of the dance you tried to get the girl to come outside, and she'd tell you to sod off and disappear as fast as she could scuttle. Like I said, necrophilia.

Anyway, by 11.30 the Magnificent Seven of us were staggering along the High Street, drunk as monkeys, yelling and shouting, having a real good time. And outside the Chinese takeaway, what do we see but this gorgeous blonde thing sitting in her car, all on her Jack Jones. Never mind that the takeaway was full of people. Never mind that there were streetlights every hundred yards. Never mind that we were all in uniform, with the regimental pride upon our manly shoulders. Oh no – just pile in. We made a beeline for the car, we tried to get the doors open, we banged on the sides, we banged on the roof, we roared filthy suggestions – she was petrified.

It didn't last for long. The takeaway door cracks open, and out shoots this bloke, her boyfriend – absolutely wild with rage, otherwise he wouldn't have been so stupid. Because to us lot, it was heaven sent. In two minutes flat, or less, he was going to be minced. The end to a perfect evening!

Luckily for him, it didn't happen. Before we'd had time to jump on him, the law arrived. A police car was spotted, on came the siren, on came the flashing light. The girl was out of the car by this time, brave lady, looking sick and holding a wheelbrace. And she must have thought she had us terrified, because we scarpered! By the time the law pulled up, we were gone.

Great night out, eh Mr Walker? Oh wonderful. So – what's the big deal? The big deal is what happened afterwards. Believe me or believe me not, it's true. The couple were arrested on the spot, taken to the station, and charged with carrying an offensive weapon, the wheelbrace.

They were both fined £15, it was in the local paper. And back at barracks, us squaddies could hardly believe it. What *I* wondered, though, was what the officers thought. I'd begun to work it out, like I said. In some ways, and for some reason, we could get away with murder. It was bloody weird, I can tell you. But you couldn't knock it, could you? Walk tall!

I got sent to Germany in the end, where you've got a lot of time to think about these things, despite what the Army would like. And over there I began to get the picture more and more, and I began to like it less and less. The problem was with Germany, was that apart from work, there is absolutely bugger all to do. Nothing. I mean, there's about a million Nato lads, all told – half of them not Krauts – and the only reason for your existence is the idea that one fine day in the middle of the night a horde of hungry Russkies are going to come screaming across the frontier to join our dole queues! And until this unlikely event takes place, you are basically a blob on a computer screen. 'This blob is our glorious Army,' reckons the Brass. 'When the great video game begins, we'll move it here, here, and here!' In the meantime – Blobsville, right? And what nationality are the women? Kraut. And what do they think of foreign soldiers? Scheisse. So what do we do about it? Drink.

If we thought we'd had great nights out on the booze in England, we hadn't been born. Over there, for the Forces, it's subsidised. It's cheap, like the snout as well, about half price. Added to which, there's damn all else to spend your money on, is there? Unless you're married or something, which most of us weren't. So you drink. And you don't have to be Albert Einstein to work out the score: you drink because you're meant to. Some crafty so and so has sat down and worked it out with a pencil, like the constipated mathematician. It's policy.

Look at it this way, Mr W. There's hundreds of thousands

of us young, fit blokes. With time on our hands and not just pockets in our trousers! If we weren't half-pissed all the time, the place would explode. What they do – and it's not just the Brits, everybody's blotto and the Yanks are sky-high on drugs – what they do is this: they keep us well-oiled, and control the explosion. If anyone goes O.T.T. they can be punished, or sent back home, or dried out in hospital, and for the rest of it – well, doesn't it work out cheap! They train up all the officers to spot the lads whose livers are about to pack up, and boast about how well they cope with alcoholism. Every now and then someone goes ape and steals a tank and mangles a few streets and dogs and old ladies on the pavement, and it may even get in the papers back home. But the suicides, and the lads broken up in car smashes, and the wife-battering on the bases – nothing.

And the fights. The other way to work off the frustrations is the fights. The key word is foreigners, and it's the same old competition crap. Nearly a million men, bored and pissed-up, and they're Krauts, and Yanks, and Frogs, and Dutchies and whatnot. Enemies. Everyone back at home's got this hilarious idea that if the balloon went up we'd fight the Russians. Bullshit. We'd fight each other. And so would they. Can you imagine what the Polacks would do if the Russkies actually gave them petrol and ammunition to put in their tanks and guns? There'd be bloody carnage, all right, but no one would ever cross the Iron Curtain. Why bother?

So by the time I got to Northern Ireland, Mr Walker, I was one cynical bloody soldier. It was all a game, it was all a laugh, it was all a bloody boring bind at times. I wasn't starry-eyed anymore, far from it, but I didn't mind it, either. It hadn't done me any harm, and I was more convinced than ever that it never would, it wasn't *serious*. Only a politician, let's face it, would be dim enough to think the Russkies *really* want to attack us, and the battles we had with the other foreign lads were more to pass the time than anything. But in Northern Ireland I came face to face with it. It all got real. The name of the caper was hatred, only it wasn't a caper. Even the little kids here hate you. They sing 'If you hate the British Army clap your hands'. And if you think – when you arrive – 'Ah, they're only kids', and give 'em a smile in return, they gob in your face. It came as a terrible shock.

The second shock is the way of life you have to lead – especially after Germany. I mean, Belfast's not exactly a place you'd want to spend a holiday in, it's not the fun capital of the Western hemisphere, but unless you're out on patrol, keyed up and carrying a rifle, you never even get to see it anyway. I'd heard about being confined to barracks, sure. But I suppose it didn't sink in. Until it happens to you, you just can't imagine what it feels like. It's like being in prison, I suppose. The Kraut birds were awful, right? As unfriendly as it's possible to be, and speaking a foreign language to boot. But after a month in barracks in Belfast I was beginning to fantasise about them. And birds back in England, birds I hadn't seen for years. Just the sight of a tit-picture in a newspaper brought me out in spots.

Confined to barracks. You imagine it. You can't go out, you can't get laid, you can't even be bothered to have a wank, half the time. You can drink with your mates, and it's like being married to them, the boredom and the frustration's terrible. There's no fun in getting drunk, even, what's the point? And if you *could* go outside, someone would try to kill you. Not like the Russkies, lurking across the Iron Curtain and full of vodka and potatoes – these bastards mean it. If you hate the British Army clap your hands.

It brings it home to you, and you begin to hate *them*, too. The Protestants are appalling and the Catholics are worse. All the soldiers say it, and you agree with them before your first week's out – we should all piss off and leave them to it.

And the bigger the bloodbath, the better. It's only the hatred keeps you going, you'd go nuts without it, because there's no rhyme or reason to it, any of it. They kill themselves, they kill each other, they kill passing nuns, and children, and anyone who gets in their way. And your mates. You get this terrible, terrible feeling of frustration.

So who's to blame for Margaret Mary Byrne? Eleven years old and shot in the head. Good and dead with a good old plastic bullet. Caught red-handed with a bag of eggs in one hand and a Mars bar in the other. Who's to blame for her?

I'd like to say, Mr W, that it wasn't me, I wasn't part of it. I'd like to tell you it was all blown up, media lies, like the authorities tend to, the Brass. But it wasn't. The truth was far more horrible than they told it on TV, appalling. And it wasn't the worst that happens over here, not by a long shot.

The death of Margaret Mary happened the day after a bomb attack on one of our patrols. It was the usual thing, a stack of explosive in a drain, set off by a wire, and it killed two of us. Yes, us. My mob. People that I knew. After you've been here a while, you get a very strange reaction to these things, and it all builds up this sense of overall frustration. The first thing you do, after the spitting, screaming rage, is to see how the Press reacts. Usually, unless it's something really big, they hardly mention it at all, the English papers, they treat it as routine. It's amazing how that hurts. You know then, honest and for sure, that no one gives a shit. Every now and again, as if to prove it, the Provos do a bombing run in London and the papers all go crazy. But if it's over here . . . Jesus. The outer darkness.

So there you are. The Provos did it, as sure as God made little apples. Or maybe it was the other lot, the Clockwork Oranges, Big Ian's nut-brigade, who knows? Who cares? It was Micks. And next morning it didn't make the front page of any so-called national rag because some bloody vicar had

72

eloped with a sex-starved choirboy or something interesting. And we were sick. Oh Jesus, we were sick sick sick. That afternoon we were called out to a riot.

I can't give you all the details, because I can't remember them. I know that four Land Rovers set off, and a couple of pigs – armoured personnel carriers, you know. I was in a Rover, and I was carrying baton rounds, plastic bullets. You're meant to shoot them at the ground, and at a good safe distance, there are rules. You *are* told though, strictly off the record, just how good a mess they can do if you aim them at a face, or a body, or even legs. Not that you need telling, naturally, but it's nice to hear it from an officer. It's nice to know they care. There were twelve of us, all told, with baton rounds. And we were in a sort of quiet rage, just sick and angry, from the day before.

You don't get many chances, over here, to get your own back. Sometimes, if you're very lucky, you get to raid the flats, or search for arms and ammo in one of the estates. Then you can show these animals what you think of them. You can smash their stuff up, and tear the pictures down and things like that, let off a bit of steam. Because they are animals, all of them, whichever side they're on. We do get briefings, sure we do, about not doing personal vendetta stuff because it only makes things worse. But nobody means it, least of all the Brass. They're only held back by the twats in Westminster, and *they'd* like to give the Micks a beating too, if they could manage it and not lose votes. I'm telling you this because it's how you feel, how I felt, in the heat of this frustration. That's how I felt. (Most of the lads, let me promise you, feel like it all the time.)

So. We come round a corner, we're not even at the riot yet we think, and there's a gang of thugs. Bottles, stones, wall-bricks, shouting. Screeching of brakes, out we pile, bang bang bang.

Let me put it another way, let me try again. We come

round a corner, all keyed up, in a state of hysteria. There's two or three youths, lounging by a wall. It's October, but it's sunny and quite warm, for a change. They straighten up when they see us, wave their arms, shout maybe. Screech of brakes, out we pile, bang bang bang. Or another way.

We come round a corner and there's a gang of kids. Maybe five or six of them, about eight or ten years old. They jump up and down, shout swearwords (so we guess, we can't hear over the engine. Or the screech of brakes). Out we jump. Bang bang bang. I hear a shout, maybe. 'That's for our mates you bastards murdered yesterday!'

And Margaret Mary Byrne is lying on the pavement, with blood leaking out of her ears. One of our lads rushes up to her, he's done his first aid, see? Then there's a million people, trying to tear his arms and legs off. Chaos and confusion. It's a riot. Next day she's dead. Baton round. Smashed her little head in. She's eleven years old.

Could it have been me, Mr Walker, who fired that plastic bullet? Or was it one of the madmen? What madmen? The day before, our mates were murdered by these savages, blown to bits. Have you ever seen bits in a bucket, Mr Walker, I suppose you never have. You wouldn't believe what it looks like when it happens, what a stomach looks like hanging from a lamp-post. And this Margaret Mary Byrne, this dark-haired little kid, was probably a Catholic. Or a Protestant. Certainly a Mick, in any case. Someone's got to take responsibility.

But it won't be me. Or any of my mates. Or anyone in England, just across the water, least of all the Government. Because, of course, we're not to blame, how could we be? We didn't start it, after all, unless you go back four hundred years, and that's ridiculous. It was these stupid Irish bastards that killed Margaret Mary Byrne, we're just here to keep the peace, to keep them off each others throats. They started it, and there's bound to be the odd innocent bystander killed, it's inevitable. They'll see sense one day, and we can all go home.

That little kid was eleven years old, Mr Walker. She'd been to buy a half a dozen eggs, and she got a Mars bar for her trouble. At the inquest the Army spokesman said there'd been a riot going on, a dozen youths in masks, at least. Everybody else said there was no riot, just some kids of ten or so, and Margaret Mary Byrne, skipping down the street. The baton round had been fired at her head, from very close, by a man all dressed up in khaki. A British soldier. No mention was made of a big nose, I'm glad to say. The Director of Public Prosecutions, after due deliberations, said there was no basis for a prosecution. Wouldn't you just know it?

If it wasn't so sad, it would be almost funny, wouldn't it? But I said we were above the law, I sussed it out, didn't I? How can we be guilty if we're the good guys? We're the keepers of the peace, the small, still voice of sanity. Despite their weird obsession with religion over here, it's pretty obvious if you think about it that God is on *our* side. And we're on his.

It was the Irish who killed Margaret Mary Byrne, of course it was. We wouldn't be here if we didn't have to be, if they'd just stop killing all the time, each other. Someone's got to do the dirty work. But I wonder what she was like, that little, skipping girl.

And Mr Walker, I wonder how *I'd* end up if I tried to get this through the post. Jesus, that'd put the cat among the pigeons. Keep up the good work though, won't you?

And better luck next time!

No Lady, Godiva

WHEN DRU BRIERLEY'S flight from Africa finally touched down at Heathrow two days late, it was hard to tell who was the more relieved – her or her parents. They had been hanging around London in an expensive hotel, ringing the airport from time to time and spending a fortune. They had been worrying as well, naturally, although they had been assured time and again that the delay did not indicate disaster. One of the anonymous voices at Heathrow, less tactful than the others – or perhaps more irritated by the monotonous regularity of the calls – had said at one stage: 'Look, it's nothing unusual. They've probably had the fuel siphoned off and they're looking for some more. It's a flight from *Africa*. Relax.'

The fuel had not been stolen, in fact, but Dru, stuck in the Dark Continent, would not have been surprised, herself. She had arrived at her departure point after a three day journey by cart and Land Rover from the bush, followed by a 500-mile flip in a Fokker Friendship. So far so good, she had thought. It had been uncomfortable, and hot, and smelly, but none the less enjoyable for that. Dru had been in Africa for two years, doing voluntary teaching in the middle of nowhere, and she was looking forward to getting back to Britain. The discomfort of the journey was relative. As far as she could remember, the seats in the aircraft were the first sprung seats her bottom had been on for more than twenty months. Discomfort? It was raving luxury!

But at the international airport, the gloss began to be rubbed off the gingerbread. She had been booked onto a London flight, of course. And all her papers were in order, naturally. And for all the good it was doing her, they need not have bothered. She was directed from one window to another, from one office to the next. But her flight did not materialise. It had disappeared off the face of the earth.

Dru Brierley was not alone in her troubles. As the hours dragged by, the departure lounge, then the car park and the dusty ground outside, gradually filled up. Not only international flights were missing, it appeared. The people who were merely hoping to hop a thousand miles or so had been left in the same kind of limbo. The Fokker Friendship on which she had arrived stood on the concrete for an hour or two, then its engines were started up. Immediately it was mobbed. Dozens of people with boarding cards, and dozens without, spilled onto the airport apron and rushed towards it. Dru did not know where it was going, but she knew she did not want it. No one else knew where it was going either – the departure and arrival boards had been immobile for weeks by the look of them. But by now many of them clearly thought that to go anywhere would be better than nothing. It took half an hour for the crowds to be dispersed. Then the plane departed, empty, for God alone knew where.

Because she could speak the languages so well, Dru – although she was one of very very few whites among the crowd – was talked to freely, and got to share the rumours. The strongest and most persistent was that the President had withdrawn the jet plane – the one that did the international flights – because he needed it for a pleasure trip. The other distant flights, by foreign airlines, had all been diverted by a safety scandal. A pilot on a German plane, out of interest, had been chatting to the airport staff about where they got the fire-fighting foam for their runway fire tenders. Some idiot, Dru was told by a wide-eyed, smiling businessman, had revealed their guilty secret – they didn't. Get any foam. The fire tenders, which raced so dramatically and noisily out onto the concrete every time a jetliner arrived, were empty. They did it just for show, and to make the European aircrews feel safe. The man had laughed. 'Imagine telling that to a German,' he said. 'Some people have no sense. Now no one will fly their planes in here, until we get some foam.' Dru didn't know if he was mocking her, or if the tale was true. She doubted it, entirely. But the story helped to while away the time.

When a jet arrived, many many hours later, Dru had to fight like mad to get a place. It was her flight, there was little doubt of that – or at least, it was a flight to London, that much had been announced. But by now everyone was desperate, and working on the theory that if they flooded on the plane, they could make it take them roughly in the direction they wanted just by weight of numbers and the collective will. Just to be on board would be enough. As one woman told Dru, she had been waiting with four young children for more than thirty hours, and they were going to see their daddy. She was getting on that plane if it was her last action. Bribes must have changed hands, because far more boarding cards than places on the plane were apparent. Some of the officials at the windows were perhaps too kind-hearted to let people down, Dru had observed. With tears in their eyes, sometimes, they had dished out cards to people going in the opposite direction . . .

It was utter chaos. It was like trying to fill a tube with toothpaste through the spout. Dru was no stranger in Africa, and race or colour didn't worry her. When some infuriated woman spat at her and called her a mean white bitch,

Drusilla spat straight back and dropped a Kiswahili insult of awe-inspiring nastiness. The woman was so shocked that she forgot herself and laughed before they were separated by the surging throng. Inside the plane Dru even got a seat – and a fat black minister of religion on her lap! Within ten minutes the jet was full. Every seat was taken, many by more than one person, and the aisle was a seething mass of furious, sweating, unhappy people. It remained like that for fifty seven minutes, by Dru's watch, until the captain's ultimatum took effect. He had announced, over the intercom, that the plane would stay there until Doomsday, if necessary. It was not going anywhere until the seats were filled, properly, by the people entitled to them. Everyone else must leave. He was African, and he said it in several tongues. When the officials boarded and checked the tickets and credentials, Dru was one of the lucky ones. The minister of religion was not. She waited until the plane was well in flight before she went to the lavatory – just in case! Better a burst bladder than someone popping out from a crack in the woodwork and pinching her seat . . . There were, after all, varying degrees of relief. She was in the air at last. She was flying. She was going home.

When she reached Heathrow, and finally came face to face with her mother and father, Drusilla Brierley shocked both herself and them by bursting into tears. She was dirty, she was dishevelled, she was exhausted, and she smelled. They were middle-aged, and immaculate, and very nervous. All three of them, secretly, had been longing for, and dreading, this moment, and the forty-eight-hour delay had not helped. When you've been separated for almost two years, and when you don't get on that well, and when you're not quite sure how the future, and being together again, are going to work out, a forty-eight-hour delay can just about put the tin lid on it. That's what Drusilla thought and felt. Likewise her mother and father.

'But Dru, you look so different,' sobbed her mother. 'You look so wonderful. Oh Dru, you look so absolutely wonderful.'

'You do,' said her father, awkwardly. And meant it. Dru, at her departure, had been a gauche and difficult girl, rather fat and dowdy, something of a trial. Now here was his daughter, back again, two years older. Quite tall, immensely brown, her dark hair sun-bleached and beautiful. Slim, tired, lean and sexy. And loving. Crying almost wildly, hugging them. Good Lord, he thought, she's so *mature*. And to think I moved heaven and earth to prevent her going. It's been the making of her.

'Dru,' he said, tenderly. 'It's so *good* to see you, darling. We've missed you so much, your mother and me. So very much.'

That night they took it easy. They drove Drusilla to their hotel, and they showed her to the separate room they'd booked for her. They left her to herself – although that was very hard to do – and they told her to have a long, hot bath, and a sleep if she wanted one. Not to worry about them, not one jot. They wanted to talk, of course they did. But they knew she must be weary, absolutely whacked. She was not to mind them, they said, she was to wind down at her own rate. If she wanted anything, a gin and tonic say, she had only to ring room service. They had ordered dinner in a good restaurant they knew for half past eight, and if it suited her they would meet her in the hotel lobby at seven-thirty. She was to dress in just exactly what she liked, to be informal, to relax. They would have a lovely meal and drink champagne.

Dru, used to nothing or a little less, used to living, eating, sleeping in the company of many others, was at first resentful. But in the bath, clutching an enormous Scotch with ice, she found herself sighing with delight. They might be funny, Mother and Pa. They might be rich and posh and pompous, but sometimes they were right. To be alone. To be in a bath. To be clean and comfortable . . . And then, lying naked in the bed. How stupid to think they did not want to talk, did not care enough to smother her. They were civilised. They were being kind, and caring, and allowing her some space. They were civilised. She smiled. And she slept.

Her new maturity – and the relief it brought her parents – was the keynote of the next few days, as it was at the celebration meal that night. From the word go she surprised them, both by her dress and by the way she behaved herself. They could not understand it, and they could not quite remember why they'd been so worried. But Dru had changed, they were sure of that. Dru had changed.

Confused they might have been, but they were quite frank about it. When they ushered her into the restaurant, her father began to laugh. When she looked at him, puzzled and suspicious, he said: 'Oh Dru, I'm not laughing at you, my dear, I'm laughing at myself. I said a "good restaurant", but it's no great shakes, this place, and as you can see, it's rather dark. Romantic, eh, with all the candles and the drapes? Your Mother and I, I'm afraid, rather thought you might insist on jeans and tatty sweater and . . . and show us up. But the food's good, I promise you.'

Dru was dressed with total simplicity – of necessity, as her wardrobe was minimal, now, to put it mildly. She had on a white dress and sandals. But the white set off her dark tanned skin perfectly, and her shoulder-length, brown-blonde hair was lovely.

'I haven't worn a dress like this for years,' she smiled. 'It'd have been more than my life was worth out there. Some of them think raping a white woman's very good for their status, believe me. At the very least I'd have been sold into the white slave trade in Tangier!'

If she was joking, they couldn't tell it, but such talk, said lightly and with no embarrassment, was a tonic to them. As the meal progressed, and Dru told them of some of her more startling experiences, the tonic became almost overwhelming. Over several glasses of champagne, she described her journey home in gruesome detail, and they marvelled, both at her fortitude and the awfulness of Africa.

'But Dru!' said her mother, giggling at the idea of her daughter sitting there, bursting for a pee with a fourteen-stone vicar on her lap, 'how did you put up with it! For two years! I'd have died!'

'Two years?' said Dru. 'Don't be silly! It was only fifty seven minutes. But when he was kicked out, it was quite a weight off my . . . *mind*, I can tell you!'

The thing was, and by the end of the evening her parents were relaxed enough to admit it to themselves, they had actually been rather terrified by the prospect of Dru's return. By their standards – and they were not right-wing, or racist, or anything like that – she was something of a firebrand politically. They had never really understood why she had wanted to do such voluntary work in the first place, and it had caused friction and unpleasantness. Of course, they had understood in the abstract – what right-thinking person would not? It was good to help people who were less well off, it was a Christian act, or duty. But if she wanted to work in Africa, they had argued, why not *South* Africa? They had friends there, distant relatives, people who would look after her. And surely she was not going to suggest (as she had done, in fact, noisily) that *they* were racist, those friends and relatives? Drusilla had been angry, and convinced. South Africa and all its works was one of the main reasons why she was going to *black* Africa. And if she could help towards the revolution, all well and good. There was going to be a bloodbath soon, and the white supremacist fascist pigs had it coming to them. It had been one of many confrontations which had left the three of them white-lipped.

Her parents' line had boiled down to this: You are young (red-rag to a bull, but there you are, how else could they phrase the truth?) and you don't know. It's very dangerous to generalise about a country until at least you've been there. Of course some things are wrong, and evil, and regrettable, but like everything else in life, it consists of good and bad, there's good and bad in everything, in everybody. And there are more, and better, ways of helping than by revolution. Violence, they always ended up, helped nobody. Drusilla merely thought them smug, contemptible.

Now here she was, at dinner in a London restaurant, being witty and dispassionate about a country she *did* know, and she was devastatingly honest. She told scurrilous and hilarious tales of corruption and inefficiency, she told sad and hopeless tales of starvation and beggary, she tried seriously to express the overwhelming *weight* of the problems. Her mother and father, tactfully but perhaps less honestly, never mentioned South Africa, nor did they express their delight at the change in her. It seemed best exemplified by her ability to laugh. After she had expressed a particularly pessimistic view of the future of the continent, her father had said slyly: 'So things are looking black in Africa, you'd say, Dru?' And she had thought that that was wryly funny.

Word of Drusilla Brierley's new 'maturity' spread rapidly through her parents' circle, and for several weeks she was content. In short, she was glad to be back. She was rediscovering England, and she was revelling in it. They lived on the edge of a fairly large town, with their house and its neighbours more or less in the country. Within seconds she could be in fields, within minutes thick woods, within less than half an hour, on open, flowing uplands. The freshness and coolness of everything was the greatest marvel for Dru, and the fantastic, universal greenness. She also loved the shops, the cars, the swarming people (although they actually lived on a rather quiet estate) and most of all the hot and cold running water. For the first ten days, if anyone wanted to find her, they had only to knock on the bathroom door.

She had to admit to herself, even in so many words, that her parents were not half so awful as she'd thought they were. They were suburban, yes, and they drove a Volvo, but she could see now that that did not make them automatically unbearable. They were prone, also, to being anti-working class, and anti-union, and read the Daily Mail, which she found abominable. They also, in their new-found confidence in her, dropped in mildly racist jokes from time to time, like referring to the Asian who had moved onto the estate as 'Singe 'is Thing'. But they did not object to him being there, truly, and pooh-poohed the idea that his presence would bring the house prices tumbling. (He was a surgeon, after all. And lived five streets away . . .) They did go on, though, about the terrible state the country was in, and the recession, and the unemployment even in their town. Which for a while, at least, Dru merely found peculiar, because everything, after Africa, was so rich, and undisturbed, and prosperous. But she did not argue. She was happy to be back.

It was a trap, of course, but by the time she started realising it, it was getting to be too late. Drusilla had been tested, and she'd passed with flying colours. Her parents' friends were invited to meals, or in for drinks at night, and Drusilla was the star turn. Gently prompted by her father, while her mother kept the gins and sherries flowing, she told and retold stories of her life in Africa, and what a revelation it had been. Dru was passionate about the country, and loved it, warts and all. To have talked about that love, to have tried to express the great things about the continent and its peoples that she had learned, slowly and with pain, would probably have counted as un-British, she thought, an embarrassment. But it took her ages to understand that it was the warts alone that made her the star turn: she was being paraded as a convert. 'She was so naive,' her mother said one night. 'But the tragedy of Africa opened her eyes, didn't it, my darling? It is *such* a tragic country.' And they all nodded, sagely, thanking God, no doubt, that there were enough whites in *South* Africa to run it properly and keep the dark at bay. While Dru just stood there, speechless, transfixed at what she'd done.

The trouble was, that within their lights they were liberals. They genuinely disliked racism, or fascism, or extremism of any sort. But they could see the complexities, they told themselves, that was the trouble. They could see the complexities in everything. At home, for instance. They could see that poverty, and unemployment, and hopelessness may have led to urban rioting, but they were adamant that violence was no answer to society's indifference. They agreed that Britain's official attitude to coloured immigration and its minority population was scandalous, but they had to concede that people were worried, and felt they were being swamped. If Dru tried to put a different point of view, however quietly, they had the complete answer to her, now: she had been away during a period of rapid change, so could not know. And she had changed her *own* mind, about Africa. She'd been converted.

Dru Brierley was back in Britain, where neither violence nor extremism washed. Unless she was prepared to risk a family disaster, unless she wanted to spoil everything – she had to join the smug consensus. It was perhaps, she thought, the price of 'maturity'.

It did not last too long, and when Dru cracked, she cracked spectacularly. It was painful at the time, but on balance, afterwards, she thought it had been worth it. Several young men in the congregation of the parish church thought so too, although her parents and their friends were mortified. When Drusilla Brierley kicked over the traces, she went the whole hog. It was amazing.

It happened on a sunny Sunday, and Dru, by coincidence, was wearing the little white dress and the sandals that she had worn on the night of her return to England. She did not normally go to church, because she no longer believed in God or ceremony, but the sort of pressure to conform she had been labouring under for weeks had been put into operation the day before, with its now predictable effect. Some special friends were coming, and it would be nice if the whole family were there, and they'd go and have a pub lunch afterwards, and so on and so on. Also, her mother had said rather archly, there was a visiting clergyman giving the sermon, and he had quite a reputation locally. He was *very* progressive, and said to be quite a dish! Against her better judgment, Dru agreed. Why rock the boat for the sake of an hour or two on Sunday morning? She had nothing else to do but lie in bed and read the papers.

The parish church was just inside the town, but set in green and spacious grounds. The congregation was small, and rather smart, and rather proud. For its size, a disproportionate number of good works were done, and money collected for the poor and needy of many lands. They did not have much, they felt, to reproach themselves with. They were quite High Church, and despite herself, Dru enjoyed the pageantry.

The visiting preacher, Mr Latimer, threw a bomb into the quiet pool that spread total consternation. He was a plumpish, handsome man of under thirty, with a comfortable, reassuring smile. Which, it soon turned out, masked a sardonic turn of phrase and mind that this particular congregation found completely unsympathetic. He made no bones about his intentions, and no apologies, either. He was attacking them. As the sermon unfolded, interest turned to shock, shock to amazement, and amazement to outrage. Two well-dressed women in hats actually forgot themselves so far as to shout objections. Drusilla was enthralled. If hecklers were allowed in church, she thought, perhaps I'll become a born-againer!

Mr Latimer's text was simple. There was a conflict, he said, between the laws of Britain and the gospel. To illustrate his point he told the story of a man called Imraz Nasool, who happened to live in their town. He was a perfectly legal immigrant, resident in Britain for more than fifteen years, whose sons still lived in Bangladesh. Despite a claim to right of entry that everyone who investigated it found absolute, the sons had consistently been refused permission to join their parents. The Home Office had lied, said Mr Latimer, and stalled, said Mr Latimer, and cheated, said Mr Latimer. As a result of the stress, Mrs Nasool had killed herself, and Mr Nasool was a broken man. In this case, he said, the law, and the way it was administered, was literally a killer.

At this point the two old ladies went into a paroxysm of rage. Their shouting was over, however – for bad as Mr Latimer was, such overt reaction was clearly deemed beyond the pale by the rest of the congregation. The visitor ended his address in silence, however frozen and tight-lipped. He ended it by pointing out that there was a petition at the back of the church, which already held two thousand signatures. He would be grateful if Christian members of the congregation would add their names to aid Mr Nasool in his struggle. The two old ladies nearly died of heart attacks, desperately suppressed.

Despite the fact that she was not a Christian, Dru Brierley was the first to sign the petition book. She was also, to her horror and amazement, the last. Her parents and their friends, looking acutely uncomfortable, hurried past her, out into the sunshine. When she shouted to them, there was an outbreak of angry shushes. You forget yourself, said one irate old fellow. You are in the house of God.

Drusilla could not wait to remedy *that* fault. She stormed into the sunlight to attack her parents. The bulk of the congregation were already there, and the hubbub was amazing. Words like 'disgusting', 'outrage', 'totally offensive' filled the air. 'Who is this man?' she heard someone demand. 'How dare he bring politics into our church? The vicar must be censured, this is unforgiveable.'

She confronted her parents, who were standing, pink and flustered, with the friends. She heard her mother saying, mildly: 'What an awful thing to do, really. One comes to church to worship.'

The family friend, the male, said: 'And such a peculiar attitude. The law a *killer*? That's just *absurd*.'

His wife, seeing Drusilla's face, said hurriedly: 'I mean, he probably has a point. We're not racialist, after all. I mean, some of our best friends . . .'

'Jesus Christ *almighty*!' shrieked Drusilla Brierley.

The crowd half turned towards her, half towards the church door, where Mr Latimer had just appeared, holding the petition book. To face the lions, Drusilla thought disgustedly; the lions of respectability.

Her anger suddenly left her, but her disgust did not. She looked at the neat little church in its green and immaculate churchyard. She looked at the congregation, so smooth, so comfortable, so self-satisfied. She looked at her parents, so palpably afraid that she might show them up still further. Respectability, she thought. That's the name of the game. Nothing's real except appearances. Nothing matters except to be approved. Nobody suffers except in the abstract, there is no *actual* pain. Respectability is their shield against reality. It is their watchword.

She thought of Africa, and a daft idea swept into her

head, unbidden. It occurred to her that she should make a gesture, a simple, silly gesture that would distance her irrevocably from their sphere, an unimportant, mildly vulgar act – to her – that they would find unbearable. She very nearly laughed. I'll show the lions what I think of them, she thought. I'll get under their pathetic little shield. And she jumped lightly on to a stone plinth, and from there to a flat-topped tomb.

Rapidly, but without a loss of grace, she kicked off her sandals, pulled her dress over her head, and stepped out of her pants. She stood on the tombstone, lithe and nude, brown and brilliant white. She smiled.

'I'm not a Christian, Mr Latimer,' she said. 'But thank you, anyway. It may not look like it, but you've brought me to my senses! This is a vote for immaturity, I'm burning my boats.'

She looked at her parents, standing at her feet. Her father had his forehead in one hand, her mother was gazing at her, white and imploring, offering her the discarded dress to cover up her nakedness. Almost everybody else was staring at the ground.

'Things are looking black in Africa, you said,' she told her father, loudly. 'And you thought it was a little joke. Well, you were right.'

The congregation, on the fringes farthest from Drusilla, started scuttling for the churchyard gates.

'But if you're not careful,' Dru went on, 'the joke will be on you. The lot of you.' She raised her voice, as the scuttling rapidly became a stampede. 'Because things are looking pretty bloody black round here,' she said. 'And I don't mean the colour of anybody's skin. Book me a ticket will you, Pa? I'm going back to sanity. To join the fight again.'

The churchyard was almost empty. Outside, the congregation jostled at the railings, looking in. It was as if she were an animal in a zoo. Drusilla became aware that Mr

Latimer was standing close, observing her. She smiled.

'What a gang of hypocrites,' she said. 'I don't know how you stomach them. They remind me of South Africans.'

Her mother gave a little whimper of humiliation and her father turned abruptly away. Drusilla bent forward and took her dress from mother. She pulled it back on over her sun-bleached head. She put her knickers in her pocket. She jumped to the ground.

'There there, Mother,' she said. 'Bear up. There are places in the world, you know, where nakedness is considered normal! Let's get to the pub, shall we? Perhaps Mr Latimer would like to join us for a drink.'

But she and Mr Latimer were standing on their own. She sighed, as her parents made for the gate. She put on her sandals. She shook her head, sadly.

'Jesus,' she said. 'Whoops! Sorry. I mean . . . well, that's going to take some patching up.' She looked at the clergyman curiously. 'You put the cat among the pigeons rather, yourself. Is that a normal reaction, old ladies doing their nuts like that?'

'Not normal, no,' he replied. 'They're usually too polite. They'd usually rather burst than break the protocol. And they responded to the disapproval of their neighbours pretty quickly, didn't they?'

'I suppose they did,' said Dru. 'Will you get into trouble? They won't unfrock you or anything, will they? The bishops or whatever?'

Mr Latimer grinned.

'I shouldn't think so,' he said. 'I imagine most people will think that one unfrocking around here is quite enough! And unfrocking me wouldn't have half the . . . visual appeal.'

Drusilla glanced at his face, startled. He was relaxed, although he did avert his eyes. A blush began to rise in her cheeks. He continued, rather more briskly.

'In any case,' he said, 'I think it has to be done, so that's that, isn't it? I'm afraid it's a very complacent society we live in. They're not bad, these people. They're no doubt Christians. But they just don't seem to know, to understand. One must never give up the struggle, I think, whatever the consequences.'

The pair of them began to walk slowly towards the gateway. Most of the people, and the cars, had gone. But Drusilla supposed her parents would be waiting, in the car park. Maybe they would not.

'I think you're right,' she said. 'I'm going back to Africa. I'd say to join "the fight" again, but it does sound rather grandiose, doesn't it? I mean, Bob Marley put it so much better!'

They walked in silence. There were birds singing in the trees.

'You don't see going back as . . . you don't think perhaps you're running away?'

She did not understand. She raised her eyebrows, quizzically.

'No,' she said. 'Just the opposite, in fact.'

'You don't think that staying wouldn't maybe be . . . more difficult? Too difficult, even? That trying to persuade your parents and their sort of people might be too hard? Too tiring? Too . . . boring?'

'I don't quite get you,' said Drusilla. But she was beginning to. Mr Latimer stopped walking, and shrugged.

'If you recognise that things are wrong here,' he said. 'That things are "looking black" in England as well as Africa, to use your joke, perhaps you ought to stay. I'm sorry, I'm being impertinent. But I assumed you took your clothes off for a reason. I imagined that you wanted to make them think, those who are capable of it. To make them realise that there's something fearful in their cosiness. Something . . . dangerous.'

'Christ,' said Drusilla, thoughtfully. 'Oh shit, sorry again. Look – I couldn't half do with that drink. Why don't we just . . .' She shook her head. 'Oh no, I'll have to go, I'll have to.

'Look,' she said. 'Taking my clothes off meant nothing to me, except as a gesture. You put it so well, all the stuff you've just come out with, that I could almost believe I'd thought it through myself. But I haven't. Yet. I just wanted to shake them, to get them off my back, to take sides again. With *you*. Do you understand?'

'Ah,' he replied. 'You're even bolder than I gave you credit for in that case! Thanks for being so frank. But I don't think we're so very far apart, you know. It was still quite moving in a funny kind of way. As well as being quite . . . enjoyable.'

The blush began again. She looked away.

'I'd better go,' she said. 'But I'm not running away, Mr Latimer, I promise you. From anything. And I will think out what you've said. I've got a lot to think about, in fact – I ought to go to church more often!

'And Mr Latimer,' she added. 'If I do decide to stay, I'll get in touch. I'd like to talk. We'll have that drink together, right?'

Suddenly she giggled.

'Do you know that joke?' she asked. 'The old one about the milkman who meets the lady in the street, and for once she isn't in her nightie? He says "I didn't recognise you with your clothes on", and her husband punches his nose! I hope you recognise me!'

They were by the gate. Drusilla walked through it. Mr Latimer stayed.

'I'll recognise you,' he said. 'Although I don't know your name, you know.'

'Oh. Drusilla Brierley. Dru.'

'Drusilla Brierley. Dru. Yes, get in touch, Dru. I'd love to have that drink. And I'm not likely to forget . . . anything.'

They smiled at each other, a little foolishly. Then Mr Latimer turned away towards the church.

And Drusilla went to find her parents.

The Ghost of Mrs Hitler

I SUPPOSE I could have said no, but to tell the truth it never occurred to me. I mean, I was a girl, and the rest of the gang was boys, and that made a difference. It made me feel quite proud, because they was prepared to take notice of me. It wasn't sex, neither, because I was younger than them, and they didn't bother about me in that way at all. Anyway, I look more like a boy than a girl. I'm dead skinny, and I like to wear my hair dead short, and I wouldn't know how to get into a skirt even if I had one. Which I haven't.

At first, when I started going around with the gang, I was scared about the raiding, and the robbing and that. I mean, I know the police don't bother much about small-time stuff, but I suppose I still believed all that rubbish my Mum used to tell me, about stealing being wrong, and so on. But you get used to it pretty fast when you're in it, like, and anyway, as Stephen said, we didn't exactly do it for badness, or because we needed the stuff. We mainly did it for the good of the country.

I laughed out loud, the first time I heard Stephen say that, because I naturally assumed he was joking. But I soon found out he wasn't. In fact he grabbed me by the wrist, then and there, on the spot, and give me a real hard Chinese burn. I didn't want to, but I had to: I screamed.

'And that's just for starters, so just you remember it,' he said. 'If you want to go with us you've got to think like us, get it? We does this for supremacy, see? We does it against the Pakis and the Yids, because we hates them. We're superior. We're the Master Race. Got it?'

I sneaked a look at Stephen's face, although I've got to admit I was almost crying, so it was blurred. He's got a nice face, Stephen. He's good-looking, with nice blond hair and he dresses dead smart. If I fancied fellas I'd fancy someone like him. But I don't. Anyway, there was no doubt, then. He was serious. He twisted my wrist some more, and I let out a kind of squawk.

'Got it, Mildred?' he said. (Yeah, that's my name, believe it or not. Can't parents be sods? But Stephen was being rotten, saying it. Normally I'm called Milly. Smaller kids wouldn't dare call me Mildred. But when someone's bigger than you, what can you do?)

'Yeah,' I said. 'Only joking, Stephen. Honest.'

Well, I kept my mouth shut for the next half hour, and just worked it out as we went along. It was the first night they'd actually let me go out with them, and it soon turned out that our 'targets' as Stephen called them, was very limited indeed. In fact, because there wasn't many foreigners at all round our way, that first raiding party was a dead loss. We did try to go in the Pakistani supermarket along by Picket Street, but the big fat bloke what kept it chucked us out before we could nick anything. I think he knew what we was up to almost before we'd got through the door.

When we was outside in the cold again, Dave and Les started to moan.

'Aw come on, Stephen,' said Leslie. 'Let's call it a day. If we're short of loot, why don't we go and do the Old Girls' shop over? They're both blind as bats and deaf as posts. We can nick some cigs and stuff there.'

'Yeah,' Dave chips in. 'That Paki's a big sod, no danger. And there's about a dozen of 'em in the back. We could get hurt.'

The other boy in the gang, Terry, was about to join in the moans I think. It was a real cold night and his nose was dripping like a tap. He was just opening his gob up when Stephen launched in.

'You gutless gang of pillocks,' he said. 'You ought to be ashamed, you did. Scared of a few wogs are you? Bloody hell, you're like a gang of fairies.'

'Anyway,' I says, trying to get back in his good books, like. 'You wouldn't really rob two old ladies, surely? They're nice, the Old Girls are. If you ask nice, Leslie, they'll probably *give* you a chockie bar!'

I thought *he* was going to have a go at me then, but Stephen give a good old laugh.

'That's right, Milly,' he said. 'You tell 'im. That's right, Les,' he went on. 'Ask 'em polite and proper and you don't need to rob a thing. Fairy!'

Terry sniffed, and a little worm of snot hanging on his lip sort of crawled back up his nose.

'Anyway, sod it,' he said. 'I'm going home to watch telly. I'm going home to bed. It's too cold out here, I'm not well.'

We all had a good jeer at him, but he had a point. It was starting to rain, sort of sleety and freezing, and none of us had coats on, naturally. We messed about, after he'd gone, but it wasn't long before we drifted back to the flats. We hung around the Dalton Street stairwell for a while, because Stephen said some Pakis might come along, but they didn't. I must've been in bed by ten o'clock. Amazing.

I went around with them all the time after that, and although there wasn't a lot of 'targets', as I've said, I got to find out that Stephen – and the others, sort of – was dead serious about not liking foreigners. My dad said it all come from Stephen's dad, who was a halfwit, but I couldn't very well ask Stephen if that was right, could I! But he went on sounding off a lot about how the Germans had got it right, and Hitler was a sort of God, and in hundreds of years time everyone would realise just what a good job he'd done clearing away the Jews and that.

We spent a lot of evenings, now it was dark early and no one could see us, painting slogans on walls all over the place. There wasn't no National Front, or none of the other Nazi lots, anywhere near us, but Stephen reckoned after a while that people would reckon there was, because of our slogans, which could only be good. He often talked about forming a branch, and becoming the local fewrer and that. I asked him what a fewrer was, being only an 'ignorant little tart' (as Dave put it) and Stephen said it was what Hitler had been. That set me off giggling, because Hitler had been a little funny-looking bloke, and Stephen was quite tall and good-looking. But when I saw the way his face went, I turned the giggle to a coughing fit.

Anyway, it wasn't long, because of there being none of them in our own area, like, before we used to go further afield. We found a couple of Pakistani corner shops, and we used to barge in shouting slogans and such, and on one good night we turned over a big pile of crisp cartons all over the floor. The old lady behind the counter come running out after us, but we was much too quick for her. We dashed off down the lane with Stephen leading the chant: 'We are the Master Race, Sieg heil! We are the Master Race, Sieg heil!' and her standing under the street lamp shaking her fist. It was great.

It was later that same evening, while we was wandering along talking about how good it had been, and if we should go back there another night, that we come across this little, dirty shopfront with the funny name over the top. None of the rest of us noticed it, but Stephen did – which is why he's the leader I suppose.

'Here,' he said. 'Dave, Milly, Les. Look at that. That name. Ain't that a Yid name, then?'

Terry spelled it out: 'M. O. N. V. I. S. Monvis. Well, it's not English, is it?'

We all stood there on the pavement, in the freezing wind. It was blowing through my trousers and top like a knife. Sometimes being in the fashion can be a swine. I'd've give my left arm to be wearing a coat just then. I had to bite my lips to stop my teeth chattering.

'No way,' said Leslie. 'That's a Jew name that is. It's got to be, ain't it? That's a Jew name, that.'

'What's he selling, then?' said Stephen. 'His window's so bleeding mucky that you can't even see through it. What's he selling, then?'

We bunched up close to the window. It was dirty, it was covered in filth. On the inside, too. There was a few old watches, and bits of junk, and a clock or two. All covered in dust and that, with the advert cards all yellow, and the piled-up boxes with pictures on them.

'The dirty old devil,' said Leslie. 'That's a Jew for sure. The dirty old devil.'

'That's it, see?' said Stephen. 'They're filth, they are. They're not fit to be in this country, straight up. They're filth.'

There was a light on in the shop, that was flowing over the backboard into the window. On the spur of the moment I said: 'Let's go in, why don't we? We can go and have a look.'

Everyone looked at each other, as if they was suddenly scared. I was freezing. All of a sudden I wanted to get inside. I egged them on.

'Come on, come on,' I said. 'You're not chicken are you? You're not scared of some old Jew?'

'It won't be open,' said Dave. 'It's late. It's nearly nine o'clock.'

I put my hand on the doorknob and turned. It opened. Just like that. There was a sharp *ding* as an old-fashioned bell went. Before the others could hold me back, I walked in. What could they do? They followed me. Like sheep. I liked that.

Inside, the shop was dead weird. It was small, and dim, and crowded out with piles of big dusty cardboard boxes. They was everywhere. Then at the back was a little counter. It was wood for about half its length, and the rest was glass. It was a display. Underneath the glass there was a load of manky-looking watches. Smelled a bit, the place did. Not of cats. Sort of like old baking. Like the school kitchens after dinner had been served. Dirty.

When the others had come in and closed the door, we stood there at a loose end for a minute or two. Nobody said nothing, and we looked around us, wondering what next. I was enjoying the warmth, but I was getting slightly nervous as well, like. Maybe this Monvis character hadn't heard the bell or something. Maybe he was deaf.

Just about then, though, we heard a shuffling. Then a door-handle turned. Then this old geezer appeared. He stood framed in the doorway for a second or two, then he shuffled into the shop.

Oh, he was a Jew all right. He was like something out of an old film on telly. He was thin, and bent, and old-looking, and he walked with a stick. He wasn't exactly small – in fact he would have been tall if he'd stood upright – and his hands and arms was quite big and muscular. But he was well crippled.

No one said nothing, even now. He shuffled forward until he was right behind the counter, under the dusty old light-bulb hanging down from the ceiling. Then he peered at us.

'Yes, boys?' he said. 'What do you want? Can I be of help to you?'

His voice was funny. You could tell he was foreign straight off. He said 'vee' when he mean 'doubleyou', and

99

his 'esses' hissed. He was wearing glasses, and he was looking over the top of them, like a lizard. The skin on his face was yellow, all in folds. And the folds was shadowy, dark and lined, as if they was full of dirt. He was horrible.

'D'you buy watches?' asked Stephen. His voice wasn't really certain, like as if he was at a loss what to do.

The old Jew peered over his glasses at him.

'Show me,' he said.

Stephen swallowed, and glanced at the rest of us. I give him a little smile.

'You a Jew are you, Mister?' Stephen said. His voice had got strong all of a sudden. He sounded proper nasty. 'You a bloody Yid are you? We're going to smash your shop up, mate.'

The old man blinked. Stephen walked right up to the counter and pointed at the watches under the display glass.

'Give me some of them watches, Yid,' he said. 'Or we'll smash your shop to pieces.'

The old man raised his left hand to his glasses and pushed them slowly up his nose. They was thick. They made his eyes look huge and funny. He stared at Stephen through them.

'Go away, little boy,' he said. 'Go away before I hurt you.'

'Right,' said Stephen. 'You bloody asked for it.'

He raised his fist above his head and smashed it suddenly down onto the display glass. But it didn't break. His fist bounced off and I heard him gasp with pain. He grabbed his wrist and tried not to let it show. His lower lip was gripped between his teeth, he was biting hard.

Leslie and David didn't know what to do. Terry made a queer noise. Then I had a brainwave.

I darted over to the door, jerked it open, and looked out. Then I put my head back in, acting scared.

'It's the police,' I hissed. 'Quick, Stephen, everybody. I heard a siren. It's the police.'

There was a rush for the door. We pelted out into the street and slammed it shut. We hared off down the darkened street and round the corner. We didn't stop for ages. We was panting fit to bust. I felt good. I'd saved the day. When we'd stopped on a piece of wasteground and got our breaths back, Stephen swore for ages. Then we made the plan. To get our own back. Manny Monvis was as good as dead.

We spent a good couple of weeks watching Manny's shop – that's what we called him, I don't know why – and it was fun because it give us something real to do. We always went there after dark, and we sussed out exactly where his windows was down the back, and which alley led to his garden, and which of the sheds was his and so on. We did it like a military op, and we never went near the front again, in case he might see us and know that something was up.

As far as we could tell – and it was ages before we was certain – the old Jew lived alone. There was no sign of any animals, even, not a dog or a cat, let alone any humans. We used to stand on the corner of the street for hours on end some nights, but we never saw no one go in the shop, neither. If he sold anything, he must've done it while we was at school, during the day. But maybe he never did. The place was filthy enough, let's face it. Maybe no one went in at all.

'He must have money, though,' said Terry, one dark night. 'It stands to reason, don't it? I mean, he's a jeweller, ain't he? All them watches and that. He must have money stashed away. I reck—'

Stephen butted in: ''Course he's got money, fool. He's a Jew, ain't he? He's a bloodsucker, it's all a rotten plot, they runs the world. But it's not that we're after. It's getting our own back. It's showing him he ain't got no right living here. This is our country, and we don't want his dirty kind. That's all.'

'Yeah,' said Terry, who was really into money, though. 'Yeah, sure it's 'cause of that, Stephen. But we'll take the money too, though? We'll grab the loot as well?'

David laughed.

'You're like a Jew yourself you are, Terry,' he said. 'We're doing it for Britain, right? Ain't that enough?'

As the time to actually do the break-in come along, though, no one argued any more. It was so exciting that no one cared *why*. We was going in. We could work out what we'd do when we got there. Only one thing – Stephen made sure we all had aerosols or magic markers on us. To do the walls with. We was going to leave our mark . . .

We had to go in late, whatever happened. Because however long we watched, Manny never shut up shop before quarter past nine, and sometimes later. After he had locked up though, he went to bed dead quick. The downstairs lights would all go off, and a top one would come on. Then it would go out about ten minutes later. We decided we'd go in half an hour after that.

The night that Stephen chose was darker than a witch's armpit, as Leslie put it. It was cold, and chucking down that freezing, slushy rain. We'd been waiting down the back alley about twenty minutes when the downstairs lights went off, and we was practically froze to death. By the time the bedroom light was switched off, the half-an-hour rule was forgotten. We left it about seven minutes, if that. He'd probably be kipping anyway. If he wasn't . . . so what?

No doubt about it, we was nervous. I felt terrified, but I reckon Terry was far worse. I'd been thinking for some time that he was looking for an excuse to slope off, before Stephen give the word to go. He kept sniffing hard, and groaning like he was in pain. I knew the symptoms: he was going to say he'd caught flu and scarper. But he left it that little bit too late.

'Right,' said Stephen. 'Off. And don't forget – when you daub the walls, don't put your torches down and leave 'em. Fingerprints, see? We can't leave no clues.'

We pushed open the crummy old back gate and crept up in the shadow of the garden wall. The ground was soft and muddy underfoot, and there was a strong smell of garbage. The wall was slimy, too, but we had to keep dead close. The centre of the garden was quite light, on account of a street lamp fifty yards away. We didn't want to risk a neighbour seeing us and calling in the cops.

When we reached the back wall of the house we clustered round beside the built-on kitchen. It was good shelter, and Les had shaded his torch special-like, so we could find a way of getting in more safer. But it wasn't even hard at all. There was a window that opened like a little door, not the sliding up and down type. The frame was rotten, and it broke dead easy. It made a noise, but not a lot. After two minutes listening, Stephen climbed in. He gently drew the bolts and unlocked the back door. Another minute later, and we was all inside, out of the freezing rain. Simple.

We moved through into a bigger room, and turned our torches on. The curtains was closed so it was quite safe. Then we just stood around and looked.

'Blimey,' whispered Terry. 'It is rough, though, ain't it?'

It was kind of, but it was kind of normal, as well. There was two big old armchairs, and a fat, squat sofa. There was a piano down one wall, which was piled all along the top with old newspapers, just like my Auntie Mim's. There was a picture on one wall, over the fireplace, a dirty old carpet on the floor, and a wooden table with dirty crocks on it.

'Well it's not that bad,' I said. 'I mean, I've seen wor—'

'Shut your mouths up, anyway,' hissed Stephen. 'Let's spread out and search the old Jew-place. Let's see if there's anything to nick or smash up.'

We all set off into the next room, flashing our torches all over. Whatever Stephen said, there wasn't no chance of us spreading out. I don't quite know why, because now we was actually *in* I don't think anyone was that afraid any more. But we was hardly relaxed, for all that.

It was disappointing. None of the rooms were spectacular, or even unusual. Just like any other pretty old, pretty dirty, house. The smell was not of filth, so much as years of dust. And dampness. I knew that smell, from one of the bedrooms in our flat. I bet there was fungus somewhere, on one of the walls. Just like at home. After a time we was making quite a noise, one way and another, but still nothing happened. Stephen squirted one or two walls with the Swastika sign, and wrote 'Yids Go Home' on the ceiling in red aerosol, but all in all it was quite boring.

Then we went upstairs. And the disaster happened.

It was David's idea, or at least he started it. He stood at the bottom of the stairwell and he shone his torch up.

'Come on, Stephen,' he whispered. 'Let's go into the lion's den.'

Terry, who was beside me, let out a little hiss. My stomach went all wobbly. Nobody moved.

'Come on,' urged Dave. 'You're not chicken, are you? Not scared of some old Jew?'

Stephen pushed suddenly past him and led the way. The stairs creaked like crazy. When he got to the top he shone his beam down and whispered: 'Come on then. Last one up's a fairy!'

That was Terry. He was trembling like a leaf. But I wasn't so far in front, neither. If I'd been a boy I reckon I'd have run. But being a girl, I had to show them, didn't I? I was sweating bullets.

We slunk into the room on the left like a gang of convicts. No one spoke much. It was a big room, twice the size of a normal bedroom, and it had no furniture. It was just full of boxes, old and dusty, nothing else. I was beginning to feel sick.

'Why don't we start a fire?' said Stephen. 'Why don't we pile them boxes up and put a match to them? That'd show the old—'

He broke off. There was a noise outside the door. A creak. It was definite.

'Oh my God!' squeaked Terry. 'Oh my—'

'Shut up!' hissed Les.

'Switch off the tor—' said Stephen.

As we watched, a thin old hand come round the frame of the door, which was open a crack. It was like a huge grey spider. It shuffled quickly sideways, and there was a click.

In the light, for a second, we must have looked like a gang of frightened schoolkids. The door opened wider and the old man stood there. He was in a long white nightshirt, and he was bent-backed as usual, leaning on his stick. He even had his glasses on, pushed right back on his nose, and his eyes were big and swimmy.

'You bad boys,' he said, in his funny voice. 'You wicked, wicked boys.'

What happened next happened so fast that I didn't catch it all. Stephen, I think, threw his torch, and it shattered on the door frame by the old man's face. Somebody - Terry I guess - let out a whimper. Then there was a mighty rush towards the door. I was swept along, I wasn't part of it, it was peculiar. I had this feeling of sort of bursting through the door, smashing into the bent old man, crashing into the bannister rail.

There was an almighty crunching sound, the clattering of feet on boards, some wild yells and the splintering of wood. Suddenly I was falling, and shouting in terror. There was an awful blow to the side of my body, then an even worse one as someone landed on me. The bannister had collapsed.

I must have passed out. When I came to, there was no noise except my own breathing. There was a buzzing in my ears, inside my head. I felt terrible. Winded. Tired. Sick. But there was something underneath me. Something white and soft. It was the old Jew man.

I lay there for a good few minutes before I tried to move. I tried to work out if all my bits was still intact, if I was in one piece. It come to me, in a rush, that I was lying on a dead body. A murdered body! And any second the police would probably arrive.

They'd left me. They'd abandoned me to my fate. My gang. My brave companions.

Trying to avoid touching the body as much as possible, I started to get up. I could see the wall in the light that spilled downstairs, and I tried to use it to raise myself, rather than press my hands into the corpse. But I couldn't move far. Something was jamming my ankle. I couldn't get away. When I found out what it was, I give a little scream. It was a hand. A bent and dirty hand. The old man's hand. He was clutching me by the leg.

All of a sudden, I was struggling. I went blind with panic. I wriggled and jerked and pulled. In about two minutes I was lying flat on my gut, stretched as far down the passage from the corpse as I could get. I'd pulled the body so that it was stretched out as well, although it was all bent up still, and I think its neck was broke. But the grip never loosened. I was sobbing with fear, exhausted. In the end I went limp, just lay there.

And the body spoke to me.

'How old are you, little boy?' it said, and the voice was hoarse and gaspy. 'How old?'

I did not make a sound. I was tense, wound up like a wire. The grip on my ankle never altered, never eased or tightened. The body sighed.

'When I was your age, boy,' the voice said. 'I lived in

Poland. When the war started I was a messenger in the Polish Army. First the Nazis overran us, then the Russians. They murdered all our officers in the forest at Katyn, and they put us into camps, the lucky ones. Until one day they freed us, and sent us South and East to join the British Army. Their allies. Their new-found allies. The British gave us sandwiches, yes I remember it, it was wonderful. Always tea and sandwiches. Then proper coats and trousers, rifles, armoured cars. They told us: "Polish men, here are armoured cars. In one month's time we go to Africa to kill the Germans. Come with us." We went.'

I lay there, not moving, like the corpse. It was strange. I wasn't scared no more, just puzzled. I wondered why he was telling it to me. It didn't make much sense. But it was crazy, though, when you thought about it, wasn't it? Him fighting in a war for us and that. Stephen said they never did, the Jews. He said they was all cowards. A daft question just popped out.

'Are you dead, Mister?' I said. 'Your neck's all bent.'

And then I noticed. The grip had eased. His hand was hardly holding me no more. I could free it easy, with a jerk. He'd let me go.

'My *body* is all bent,' he said. 'In North Africa my armoured car was blown up. But I had killed my Nazis. It was enough. Little boy? Why are you so foolish?'

'I'm not a boy, I'm a girl,' I said. I felt all ashamed, it just rolled over me. 'I'm not really in the gang,' I said. 'I just hang around with them, sort of. I didn't mean to hurt you.'

He made a noise that could've been a laugh.

'Well,' he said. 'That will comfort me.' He took his hand right off my ankle. 'Go now, little girl, I want to rest.'

'I'll get a doctor,' I said. 'I'll call an ambulance.' I stood up, shakily. I hurt all over. But I didn't care. I felt terrible, I had to call in help.

The funny noise came again.

'Fascist turned Good Samaritan,' he said. 'It is not a likely tale.'

I didn't know what he meant, exactly, but I could work it out. He was telling me to sod off.

'But you'll die,' I said. 'It's cold and horrible. You'll die.'

He opened his eyes, and they sort of wandered round until they found me. He put his hands up, like as if to move his glasses, but he stopped. They'd gone.

'Yes,' he said. 'I will die. But not today. Or tomorrow, either. Hitler could not kill me, little girl. It is not much chance that you and your friends should do so, huh? Your baby fascists and their little hanger-on!' He paused. 'Hitler had a hanger on,' he said. 'Did you know that? Her name was Eva Braun. He agreed to marry her on the day he killed himself like a dog. So that her name, also, could stink in history with his.'

His eyes closed. He looked sort of peaceful.

'Mr Monvis,' I said. I blurted it out. I had to help him, he had to let me help him, it wasn't fair. 'Mr Monvis!'

'Tell your friends, my little hanger-on,' he said, 'that Hitler lost the war. It is the thing his admirers always forget, because they have to. Sieg heil was their slogan, and Hitler lost the war. Sieg heil! That is funny, huh?'

I knelt beside him. I'd said it often enough, we all had. But I'd never knew what it meant, for all that. Neither had the others, I realised. Or they'd've told me. But I couldn't ask him, could I? I couldn't bear to. I put my hand out and touched his face. And he opened his eyes.

'Eight million Germans dead, and a stink in the nostrils of history,' he said. 'That is what he gave them, that was his great gift to Germany. It is what happens to fascists. All of them. Always.'

He smiled.

'And you,' he said. 'Are a hanger-on. Like little Eva Braun. Sieg heil.'

The smile faded away, although the eyes stayed open. I opened my mouth to speak, but changed my mind. I took my hand off that folded, yellow face, and stood up.

I went and called an ambulance.

A Pitiful Place to Die

UNTIL THE VERY moment of disaster, David Lowston knew he was unique. Sitting at the wheel of the assault boat, his right hand flicking the throttle lever now and then as a heavier grey sea rolled under the lean grey craft, he felt superb. The weather was horrendous, and the small amount of flesh that was not protected by his heavy-weather gear was numb. In a minute or two, or half an hour – anytime – they would be off. Lieutenant Parsons, who sat beside him, would give the order, and he would hit the throttle, hard. The thin light alloy boat would bury her stern in the freezing South Atlantic, and Pryke and Hanson, enveloped in their tarpaulin with the vulnerable equipment, would get much wetter yet. After that, the killing would commence.

Lucky me, thought David, smiling through the spray that burst into his face. Stuck down here on the edge of the antarctic winter, a million miles from nowhere, doing exactly what I always knew I wanted, exactly what I always knew I'd do. I've made it to the élite of the élite, I'm one of the crème de la crème. A seaborne soldier, a secret hero, a boat service man. Waiting for the off. A nasty, coaming sea came roaring in across the line he was keeping on, and he flipped the throttle and the wheel. Somewhere out there, in the spindrift and the mist, was the enemy, the prey. God help those poor bastards!

Beside him, Lieutenant Parsons cupped his hands over his

face and appeared to speak into his radio, although no words were audible. David glanced beyond him, to the next assault boat, some twenty yards away. It looked absurdly small and vulnerable, always half-awash in white, flowing water. His mate Ted Phillips was on that one, part of Captain Cameron's team. They had a bet on, he and Ted, to see how many Argies each could kill, if they got the nod. Ted had no chance. And out of sight, he knew, around the headland, there were other boats and other men, all determined to do better. It was an exciting time.

David Lowston did not know the exact strength of their little force, nor did he know their exact target. Because *they* were involved, however, the boat service élite, he guessed it would involve an assault on a ship or submarine that was not a sinking job – the Navy could do simple work like that. There must be a necessity to take out a crew and keep the vessel. Almost certainly, he reckoned, to do with codes, or secret electronic gear. There would be resistance, and danger. And the chance to go in hard.

As a bigger, more vicious wave tried to push his boat askew, he reflected that the weather was deteriorating, if that were possible. From appalling to bloody unbelievable! Funny to think that back at home the sun was probably shining, and people were lying on the beach. They only existed, any more, in his imagination, and he – if he existed at all – in theirs. He thought of Carol, and of his mum and dad. The summer people, going about their normal lives and knowing only that he was down here fighting for them, and his Queen and country. A bank of blinding, freezing fog came rolling in towards them, from the sea. Shit, thought David Lowston. But he also felt a fantastic rush of pride. And *joy*. As Captain Cameron's boat disappeared from view, as visibility dropped to almost zero, he was overcome by a blazing sense of worth, of belonging, of glory. This was living, and he was unique.

The disaster struck then, at that very moment, and no one in the boat ever knew what caused it. Perhaps enormous seas had rolled in with the fog, one of the screaming white squalls they had learned to expect from time to time. Or maybe the secret enemy had struck, had sussed them out, outflanked them and destroyed. All Lowston knew, for the short while that he knew anything, was that his cold, wet world had blown apart. There was concussion, a hammer-blow then many hammer-blows, and noise, and freezing, flooding seas. His eyes, mouth, nose, ears, everything, were packed with solid water. Water like lead, heavy with pressure. He thought his eyes would burst, or be collapsed. He thought that he was flying, in a mighty tumble-drier. He was whirled about and battered, ripped bodily from his boat and smashed. Then there was silence, and solitude. Nothing.

David Lowston was not unique, he was just another soldier; hardly an élite, another casualty of war. It took him many minutes to come round, because the pain of his injuries was part of a more general pain, the pain of freezing. He was first aware of consciousness through pain, he first realised he was injured, then later that he must, because of this, still be alive. He had been awake, aware, alive, for what seemed eternity before he opened his eyes, and then saw little. About an hour later he felt well enough to groan. A torch was shone at him, and he heard a voice.

The voice came as a shock, because ever since he'd drifted into life, his world had been filled with a louder, roaring din, that had been at once distant and close. The voice was intimate, and it put the background noise into context, suddenly. He recognised it as the sound he'd lived with for many weeks, the song of the South Atlantic. Outside his small existence, a storm was blowing.

For many hours after this, David Lowston drifted in and out of life, only vaguely knowing what was going on. At times the pain was appalling, hardly bearable. At other times, he sensed, rather than felt, the magic needle going in, the morphine flooding through his veins, enabling him to take some sort of stock. He was lying on a bed of stone and oilskin, and his left leg, trousered still, was stretched in front of him. His right leg had a boot on, and at the bottom and the top was clothed. But at the knee, from the lower thigh to the upper shin, it was sometimes bare when he focussed on it, sometimes covered. When it was bare it was appalling. Through the muscle and the flesh poked ends of bone. Cracked and splintered, white with shreds of meat attached. Oh, what a vivid mess. Then later on, the leg had disappeared, first under bandages, and then his trouser leg, pinned loosely back together. It would not pass a passing out inspection, thought David Lowston, passing out.

Much later, David Lowston was awake, aware enough to take in his surroundings. He was lying alongside his mate, Ted Phillips, and he heard the voice once more. The voice said to him, soft but clearly: 'Are you awake, old son? Thank Christ for that. You're going to be all right, no worry, right?' Of course I am, thought David Lowston. Where the bloody hell am I?

He was in a hut, it transpired. An ancient hut they'd found on the beach. God only knew how long it had been there, or who had built it, but Lieutenant Parsons, who loved and revered knowledge and old things, thought it was a relic of the sealing days, a makeshift shack that must have been built as a shelter by some poor shipwrecked bastards. Until, if they were lucky, their mates or someone else came into the empty, shallow bay and rescued them. It was built of driftwood, he pointed out, most of which was from wooden ships. Deck planks, and hull strakes, and fragments of smoothed, rounded timber, masts and spars. What David Lowston was not told, nor Ted Phillips either, was that there were other bones in evidence, not just the bones of ships. On the frozen ground that made the floor were human bones,

113

that Parsons and the other able-bodied men had cleared into the snow outside.

There was another strange circumstance which Parsons knew, and which – perhaps unthinkingly – he let slip out. He looked at David speculatively and asked him: 'Were there any sealers in your family, Lowston, way back in the old days?'

David blinked, it was a crazy question.

'No sir, not that I was ever told of, anyway,' he said. Then a pause. Captain Cameron said: 'Why, Andy? What are you driving at?' But Lieutenant Parsons, hunched into his hooded parka, was disinclined to answer. He shrugged. 'Oh nothing much,' he said. 'Just an odd memory, that's all.'

'What, sir?' said David. 'About me, sir? What do you mean?'

Despite himself, there was a note of pain in his voice. It was beginning to eat through the morphine, in vicious, probing bites. Lieutenant Parsons put a hand on his arm, reassuringly.

'No, not about you,' he said. 'There's an old sealing song, that's all, and it's about a chap called Davy Lowston. "My name is Davy Lowston, I did seal, I did seal." That's the first line. Coincidence. Weird, eh?'

'Oh', said David. 'Nice to know there was some other poor sod down here suffering, then. How did he make out?'

Parsons' face was hidden by his fur-lined hood.

'They must have been hard men, those,' he said. 'Can you imagine it, whaling and sealing a hundred years ago and more. No engines, no heat, no thermal underwear. To come all this way, of your own free will, to work. Bloody heroes.'

Pain was biting into David Lowston's leg. He could feel sweat breaking out, then chilling, on his face.

'How did he make out, this Davy Lowston, sir?' he repeated. Parsons made a head movement within his hood.

'Do you know, Lowston,' he said. 'I can't remember the

114

song at all. Only that first line. "My name is Davy Lowston, I did seal, I did seal".'

There was a pause, silent except for the howling wind.

Captain Cameron said: 'We'd better forget the glee club in any case, chaps. Able-bodied men outside to get more driftwood for the fire.' David Lowston felt his consciousness slip away.

The able-bodied men were these: Lieutenant Andrew Parsons, in charge of Lowston's boat, who had suffered a broken finger and two deep gashes to his face. Captain Ewan Cameron, in charge of the other craft, who was not injured. Albert Lightfoot and Arthur Swanley, stern-men with Captain Cameron, of whom Swanley was unscathed and Lightfoot had a broken arm. The dead were both from Parsons' boat, and they were the stern-men Hanson and Pryke. His driver, David Lowston, had a shattered leg, and Cameron's driver – Edward Phillips – was dying visibly. He had two broken legs and probably a broken back. He also had an odd cast to his eyes, that suggested that his skull was fractured, and had been twisted out of shape. If they had had enough morphine to spare, the two men in command would have killed him off, for all their sakes, including his.

There was no doubt, incidentally, that Hanson and Pryke were dead, and had not drifted off to land somewhere else, or been picked up, perhaps, by other power-boats in the team. For all the soldiers on the operation wore life-jackets, guaranteed to float them, and float them, what is more, with their bodies upright and their chests and heads well clear. In the first dawn after the disaster, Pryke and Hanson had come ashore, nodding vigorously, as if they had intended to walk straight up the beach. Except that their faces were grey, and waxen, and sheathed in ice. More chilling still, to Cameron and Parsons (who kept it very quiet) was that the day after that, as they stared through the flying spume that screamed across the broken wavetops, they saw six other doll-like forms swaying in the spray as they drifted slowly southwards on the tide.

There was one other thing that Cameron and Parsons intended to keep quiet, for they judged their situation pretty bad already, and they did not want a mystery, or hysteria, to shatter what morale they could still hope for in the team. They talked about it late one night, when they were keeping watch, and everybody else was either unconscious or asleep. Or so they thought. They talked in darkness; and against the howling background of the night, they thought, their chances of being overheard were nil. But David Lowston overheard them. Or perhaps he only dreamed it. Perhaps what followed was illusion.

Whether it was real or not, he heard the lieutenant and the captain speak his name. The lieutenant talked of the coincidence of the song, and explained why he'd clammed up when questions had been asked. 'Poor old Lowston,' he said. 'In truth, Ewan, I couldn't sing the rest. Even the first stanza's bad enough.' He sang gently, in the glow from the driftwood fire. 'Oh my name is Davy Lowston, I did seal, I did seal, Oh my name is Davy Lowston I did seal. Though my friends and I were lost, and our very lives it cost, We did seal, we did seal, we did seal.'

'Yes,' said Captain Cameron. 'Heavy. Is it a true story, or what?'

'God only knows,' replied the lieutenant. 'If it's not exactly true it'll be the distillation of plenty that was. Those sealers' lives must have been two a penny. Can you imagine it, honestly? To come ten thousand miles in a sailing ship to work from this God-forsaken spot. They must have been desperate.'

'Well,' said Captain Cameron. 'I suppose they had a choice. There must have been other ways of getting a living. Misplaced romanticism, I expect. Better than driving an ox-cart down the lanes of Hampshire, maybe. And someone

116

must have got some glory out of it, even if it was only the people who owned the ships!'

Andrew Parsons laughed.

'Still people mad enough to come here,' he said. 'Not just us, either. There's a couple of dozen all the time, scientists and nutters of one kind or other, living on chocolate bars and penguin shit. It's beyond me.' He reached forward and threw another piece of driftwood onto the fire. 'Anyway,' he said. 'Thank God your name's Cameron, and not McGrath. He was Davy Lowston's skipper, and he set out to sail to Port Stanley to get help, poor devil. Eight hundred miles, in a bloody open boat. Heroes, all of them. Or madmen.'

'Wouldn't be much percentage in sailing to Stanley now,' said Cameron. 'Just think of the reception committee! What a feat though. Eight hundred miles across this lot, this awful bloody ocean. Did they make it?'

David Lowston, in his dream or his delirium, waited. There was a long pause. Then Lieutenant Andrew Parsons softly sang a verse.

Our captain John McGrath he set sail, he set sail.
Oh yes, for old Port Stanley he set sail.
'I'll return men, without fail.'
But he foundered in the gale.
And went down. And went down. And went down.

Captain Cameron did not comment. David Lowston, if he had not dreamed it, slipped into oblivion.

For the next two days, the ice survivors lived in a limbo of hope, and cold, and inactivity. They collected driftwood, and conserved their food, and they talked – when they talked at all – of how they would be rescued, and by whom, and when. The hours dragged by into days and no one came, but they never suffered from despair. This was a modern age, an electronic age, and the point at which they'd disappeared was known. Someone would come, and it would not be long. They did not despair. Officially.

They had a radio with them, and they had a few supplies, and enough warm gear – coupled with the ancient shelter – to keep them just alive. They had a compass, what is more, and they had an outline map. The map, unfortunately, indicated that the bay they had fetched up in was ringed with impassable cliffs of rock and ice. But they did not trust it much, because the shelter, although large enough for six of them, was not marked. In truth, they thought (and life was full of little ironies) they were probably within a mile or two of what passed for civilisation on this group of frozen rocks.

And what did? Just what were they down there fighting to regain? There was an old abandoned whaling station, that much they all knew, because the war had started when a party of scrap metal men had landed to dismantle it – and run up a foreign flag instead. And presumably, there were now the interlopers, in force, with huts, and food, and shelter. Then there were the scientists and loners, the men and women who chose to come, to watch the cloud formations and the seabirds whirling round. They must have food and shelter, too. 'If we were birds,' said Albert Lightfoot, 'they'd beat a pathway to our door, God damn them.' 'Yeah,' said his oppo, Swanley, laconically. 'And clip a name-tag to our ear'oles before they set us free!'

Captain Cameron said: 'There might be our own chaps by now, you know. For all we know, men, the islands could be swarming with us. Our best bet is just to wait, to keep on plugging away on the radio set and hope. A signal might be going out, even if nothing's coming in. We'll be rescued soon enough.'

Everybody nodded in the approved military manner, including David Lowston, who was fully conscious for the present, not even in much pain. Everybody nodded except Ted Phillips. While they had been taking stock he'd died. It was not noticed for another hour.

That night, in agony from the leg that was slowly going

118

black, in anguish at the death of his friend, and with an extra
dose of morphine that the same death had released for him,
David Lowston slid into a combination of black despair and
wild hallucination. The half-imagined, half-heard tale of
long-dead sealers was part of it, but heroism was the theme.
How can this have happened to us, he asked Lieutenant
Parsons in the dream. How can we be here, wrecked and
dying on the beach? How can Ted be dead? We're the best
in the world, we're the crème de la crème. I'm depressed as
buggery, sir, but how can that be true? Can supermen get
depressed?

He knew it was a dream, because Lieutenant Parsons was
dressed as Superman, except that bones were sticking lividly
through his sleek blue tights and his eyes were bent and
funny like Ted Phillips's had been. Lieutenant Parsons
spoke.

'It's all a myth, this killing seals, young Lowston,' he said,
and he spoke in Phillips' voice. 'You're down here freezing
to death and Carol's lying on the beach in her bikini with
the hots for someone else. Who will she stay with tonight, I
wonder? Not with you, for sure. You useless bastard, look at
you. That's frostbite, son, that blueness. And what's the
smell in here? Gangrene setting in. You're bolloxed, Davy
Lowston. Knackered, my old son. You're finished.'

David Lowston writhed. He moaned. Superman turned
slowly back into Lieutenant Andrew Parsons. His voice
became smooth and cultured.

'You mustn't worry about it, Dave,' he said. 'We're only
human beings, actually, not supermen. And Superman
himself was just a spotty-faced reporter in a comic
originally. He couldn't even make it with his girl. It's all a
put-up job, this heroism lark. Nobody really gives a shit. It's
only just a legend. It makes the folks back home feel
comfortable about sending us out to die.'

David Lowston groaned. He shouted, as if through cotton

wool: 'But I'm in it for the glory! I'm killing seals for glory, glory, glory.'

A voice from nowhere said: 'Only the masters of war win glory. The dead look on. Do not ask questions, just rejoice.'

He came to, screaming. Before he received oblivion from another jab, he heard Ewan Cameron say to Parsons: 'If he can still scream he's still alive. But not for long. I'm going out tomorrow, Andrew. I'm going to do a Captain John McGrath.'

The boats were both still on the beach, and one of them was smashed beyond redemption – recognition almost. They were light, fast, built of strong thin alloy, expendable. The smashed boat's outboard was intact, but it would not start. Its electrics were soaked through. Neither of the tool-boxes had survived, and without tools the vital parts could not be brought to the fire to be dried. Captain Cameron was determined, though, and he worked throughout the brief hours of one short day with Swanley and Parsons. Lightfoot tried to help, but his broken arm was hurting constantly and he was becoming very weak. It was another reason for Cameron to go. The chances of survival for the group were dwindling. The unfit men would die soon, the fit soon afterwards.

The floatable boat was stripped of everything that was not considered necessary to the venture. One paddle was found intact, and a piece of flattened alloy was beaten into shape to be used as another. Captain Cameron and Lieutenant Parsons, after consultations that they kept secret from the rest, distributed the remaining rations. Cameron was taking Swanley as his crew – he was the only man capable of sustained effort except Parsons, who being an officer had to remain. They took the compass, and the map, and provisions for about one day. There were no plans to do a John McGrath in *fact* – far from attempting eight hundred miles they hoped only to clear the headland and set a general compass course for the settlement downwind. They would paddle to begin with, and to push the boat in when they needed to make a landfall, but the wind, and the current with some luck, would be their motive power. Lieutenant Parsons and Albert Lightfoot helped them launch and waved them off.

As if by some miracle, the weather cleared up for the launch. The gale that had started blowing when disaster struck, and had continued to howl whitely for days, died away as suddenly as it had begun. Half an hour before the launch, it was screaming into the shallow bay, freezing and vindictive. But when they manhandled the vessel into the surf, the sky was blue and clear, the water bright green and beautiful. Not still though – still water was a desperate rarity in these latitudes. They shipped some rolling seas as they fought out through the surf, and Lightfoot and Parsons, pushing up to their waists, were soaked to the skin, through the layers of PVC, and oiled wool, and silk. When the boat was several yards offshore, clear of the breaking crests, the two of them saluted in the sunshine. The two men in the boat, also soaked and already half exhausted, waved back. The scene was oddly beautiful. After half an hour the boat was out of sight, round the headland, drifting quickly South.

That night two things happened, one not unexpected, the other a dreadful shock. The predictable thing was the weather. At dusk the air was almost still, the fading light still brilliant. Half an hour after dark the next storm struck. With it came snow, and a wind-power greater than any of the last few days. The sealers' shelter, which had stood for God knows how long, shook and rattled horribly. It did not give way, though. Packed with rock and ice, built of stout timber and lashed with hemp, it would probably last for ever. But Albert Lightfoot, unable to recover his body heat after launching the boat, weakened by the draining agony of

121

his splintered arm, died. Quietly, although not asleep. Lieutenant Parsons, who had been listening to his stoic efforts to suppress the noise of pain, heard him give in and slip away. David Lowston, on the other side of the fire, was babbling and groaning through his nightmares. Lieutenant Parsons, desolate, sucked in his cheeks and bit the inside of his mouth.

Before Lowston died, he had a period of lucidity. It happened after Parsons had returned from disposing of Lightfoot's body outside. The weather was clear once more, the sun was shining, the air was motionless. Parsons entered through the shelter door and jumped when Lowston spoke to him.

'They're dead, sir, aren't they?' said David Lowston. 'The captain and Art Swanley? Just like in the song.'

Lieutenant Parsons sat down and rubbed his left hand across his eyes.

'What song?' he said, tiredly. 'You don't know any song, old son. Neither do I. Don't think about it. Just keep your strength up till they bring help.'

Lowston tried to sing, but he only quavered.

'"I'll return men, without fail".

But he foundered in the gale.

And went down. And went down. And went down.'

Lieutenant Parsons sighed.

'I thought you were asleep,' he said. 'Or unconscious. I never knew you'd heard me singing that.'

'It's a good song, sir,' said David Lowston. 'Pretty sad, though. Is that the end of it?'

'I don't remember.'

There was a long, long silence. Only the crashing surf. No wind.

'I wonder why they did come here to seal,' said David Lowston. 'Because they were mad? To prove how tough they were? To make themselves rich? Poor bastards. I bet the only people they made rich were the sods back home, in their great big country houses. Bastards. And what happened to the sealers? Nothing. Bugger all. Oblivion. I'd never have heard of them if you hadn't known that song.'

'At least they had a song,' said Andrew Parsons. 'I'm a bit like you I think, David. I dreamed of glory. But no one will ever know about us, not until years later, maybe, in some history books. When the nasty little odds and sods come out. The black side of the game. It's heroes who win votes, heroes and living men, not cripples and corpses. This shitty little war will be forgotten when there's no more votes in it, but we've been forgotten already. The unknown soldiers, disappeared on active service. Which anyway would not be talked about. We're hardly unsung *heroes*, after all, even if we're unsung. Cutting sailors' throats, old son. That's what we were going to do, for the glory of old England. Just like dirty murderers.'

'Just like killing seals.'

A long, gentle breath of wind flowed around the shelter. Outside, the sky was darkening. Soon there would be another freezing storm.

'I'm twenty four,' said Andrew Parsons. 'How old are you?'

David Lowston did not reply for some minutes. His eyes were misting over.

'I'd be nineteen soon,' he said. 'Is that the end of it? That song. Sing me the rest of it, sir. It's getting dark.'

Andrew Parsons sang. Outside, the wind was blowing up. A burst of spray flew up the beach and rattled on the hut.

'So come all ye lads who venture far from home,
Far from home.
Come all ye lads who venture far from home.
Where the icebergs tower high,
That's a pitiful place to die.

Never seal, never seal, never seal.'

David Lowston's eyes were closed. Lieutenant Parsons put some more wood on the fire, gently.

And lay down beside him.